The Miles Between

The Miles Between

Mary E. Pearson

Henry Holt and Company

NEW YORK

Henry Holt and Company, LLC
Publishers since 1866
175 Fifth Avenue
New York, New York 10010
www.HenryHoltKids.com

Library of Congress Cataloging-in-Publication Data
Pearson, Mary (Mary E.)
The miles between / Mary E. Pearson.—1st ed.
p.   cm.
Summary: Seventeen-year-old Destiny keeps a painful childhood secret
all to herself until she and three classmates from her exclusive boarding
school take off on an unauthorized road trip in search of "one fair day."
ISBN 978-0-8050-8828-1
[1. Secrets—Fiction. 2. Emotional problems—Fiction.
3. Friendship—Fiction. 4. Boarding schools—Fiction.
5. Schools—Fiction.] I. Title.
PZ7.P32316Mi 2009   [Fic]—dc22   2008050277

First Edition—2009 / Designed by Meredith Pratt
Printed in the United States of America

1   3   5   7   9   10   8   6   4   2

For Dennis and the magic, with my love

The Miles Between

1

I WAS SEVEN THE FIRST TIME I was sent away. This raised eyebrows, even among my parent's globe-trotting friends, and I was brought back home in short order. Rumors are embarrassing, you know? A nanny was employed, but that only partially solved their problem. I was still in the house. I was seen and heard. When I turned eight years old, it seemed reasonable to send me off again. And they did.

They never kept me at any one place for long. The counselors are bothersome and have too many requests. Like asking that my parents visit at least once. Or that I return home for holidays. When rumblings begin, I know I will be shuttled off somewhere new once again. I don't allow myself to get too settled or attached. There is no point.

I came to Hedgebrook when I was fifteen. That was almost two years ago. It is by far the most beautiful of the boarding schools I have attended. I commend Mother and Father. Rolling green hills hem in the redbrick mansion that serves as the school. Many of the dorm rooms still have bars on the windows, due to its previous use as a mental hospital, but they don't interfere overly much with the view from my room. I can see pasture after pasture, white fences that bend and hide with the hills, two red barns, and a farmhouse that is so far away I can only guess that the color might be blue.

Today is October 19, the exact same date I was sent away when I was seven. I pay attention to dates, numbers, and circumstance. Obsessively, some say. I prefer to think of it as careful observation, finding the pattern to coincidence. Can there really be such a thing as a pattern to coincidence? It would seem to defy the very definition. But many things are not what they seem to be.

Take Hedgebrook, for instance. Hedges are abundant here. They separate gardens, stables, and fields. Some are large and loose, and move in the wind like sheets billowing on a line. Others are small and tight, like nervous turtles hunched in their shells. And others in the distance, naturally sprung up along brooks and in the dips of hills, are really a mixed batch of trees and shrubs, actual forests if you could get through them, but hedges by default.

And then there are the brooks. There are four within a short stroll of Hedgebrook. They all tie together somewhere, I'm sure, or maybe they all started out together once and were separated by an unforeseen knoll, but they thread around Hedgebrook like thin shoelaces, so there is always some babbling within earshot.

But it is only coincidence, for it is not the hedges or the brooks for which Hedgebrook is named but for Argus Hedgebrook, who built the first home here in 1702. Not a tremendous coincidence. Some would say none at all. But still, I think about it and wonder, like I wonder about today.

I snap my sheet as I have done every morning since I have been here. Schedules are the lifeblood of Hedgebrook. Failure to follow the prescribed routine has consequences, and I am resigned to that because, really, Hedgebrook is a place I can sink into. I wouldn't say I love it, but I can feel invisible, which is not such a bad thing to be. It fits around me comfortably, like my gray chenille robe. But mind you, I am not attached to Hedgebrook. I wouldn't be so foolish as that.

My aunt Edie visits every three months. It is not easy for her. As rich as my parents are, she is poor. Not destitute poor, but traveling is a luxury for her. She tried to get custody of me when I was ten, but I suppose she couldn't outmuscle my parents' lawyers. Nothing came of it. But every time she visited, she would tell me she loved me, and every time I would ask why my parents wouldn't let me live at home, and every time she would turn away and wipe at her eyes. I don't ask her anymore. I enjoy her visits, and I don't like to see her cry. Crying is something I avoid watching and doing. Nothing comes of it either. I learned that when I was seven.

The breakfast bell rings, and I hear shuffling in the hall outside my door.

"Breakfast, Des," Mira says, briefly poking her head in the door, before she hurries on.

Like I don't know.

Mira's daily reminder drove me mad at first. I punched her on my fourth day here. Impulsive, yes, but I hadn't quite settled in yet. I thought it would stop her, but the next day, there she was again, announcing breakfast, and I realized that perhaps she couldn't help herself. Well, certainly she couldn't, if even her swollen lip was not a deterrent. And she didn't tell anyone how she got it either, so I tolerate her daily intrusion, thinking of it as a newspaper smacking my door. I've even added to the routine with my daily response.

"On my way, Mira." It's a small thing to offer for one who doesn't cry over split lips.

I tuck the sheet beneath the mattress and quickly tuck in the blankets as well, neatly folding the corners, the way Aunt Edie showed me years ago. She comes after classes today for a two-day visit. Mrs. Wicket knows that Aunt Edie is low on funds, so she allows her to stay in an empty room over the old carriage house. It is against the rules, but Mrs. Wicket likes Aunt Edie, and I suppose she likes me, though I have no idea why. I make a quick phone call to the front office to remind them of my aunt's pending arrival and then comb my short black locks with my fingers and a sprinkling of water from the glass by my bedside.

Before I leave for breakfast, I take a last look at my calendar. My days are bunching up. I have never been anywhere this long. I know the news will come soon. Where will they send me next? But it is best not to think about it, because that means I would care, and I don't. I rip October 19 from the pad and crumple it into the trash. It feels almost illegal to dispense with a day that hasn't yet played out. I smile at the thought of being able to so easily control my destiny.

2

"THE OATMEAL IS PASTY TODAY."

I plop three ladlefuls into my bowl and pour milk on top. Of course it is. The oatmeal is always pasty. Mira is a fountain of old information. But I give my usual lengthy response so she won't repeat herself.

"Hm."

The dining room is emptier than usual. There are three dining rooms at Hedgebrook: the larger hall that holds all 420 students and the two smaller ones off the kitchen. I eat in the smallest one most often, along with eight or nine other students. The room is furnished simply, with one large no-nonsense wooden table and a dozen sturdy chairs around it. I set my bowl and glass of juice down.

Curtis and Jillian are on either side of me. Mira, Aidan, and Ben are opposite us. Mrs. Wicket sits at the end reading the paper with one hand, nibbling buttered toast with the other, and trying to talk to students as they arrive. The true definition of multitasking.

"Good morning, Destiny."

"You shouldn't talk with your mouth full, Mrs. Wicket," I tell her.

"Yes, I know. You've told me. Sleep well?"

"Where is everyone?" I ask, meaning the usuals. I try to stir the lumps from my oatmeal, and milk spills over the side of my bowl onto the table.

"Isabel is sick. Seems to be a mild case of the flu, but just the same we've isolated her in her room," Mrs. Wicket answers.

"She never gets sick," Jillian says.

"Today's her recital, too. Why today of all days?" Mira adds.

Ben shakes his head and only says, between mouthfuls, "Bad timing."

I look out the window and feel something stirring, not on my skin but somewhere deep inside. A blast of wind and leaves hits the window, startling Mrs. Wicket so that she drops her toast on her plate. "Goodness! Where did that come from? The forecast today called for fair weather."

"I could have told you," I say, stirring in another spoonful of sugar to make the lumps more palatable. "It's the nine-teenth."

"Oh, boy, here we go." Aidan leans back in his chair. "Don't indulge her."

"And what does the nineteenth have to do with wind?" Jillian asks.

"It's only breakfast talk, right, Des?" Mira offers.

"Nothing," I tell Jillian. "But certainly there will be nothing fair about today, including the weather."

"Profound. Can we stop now?" Aidan is fearful of any-thing fateful or coincidental.

"I'm just saying—" No need to frighten them all. And saying one more word might do it. I know the tics and fears of each person who sits in our dining room. I know how they cross their feet beneath the table and how much food they leave on their plate each morning. I know how often they look askance at the others and how often they wonder if they are being noticed. I know how often Jillian will touch her napkin to her lips—twenty-two times— and how many times Curtis will clear his throat— seventeen times—like he is trying to find the courage to speak. I know how many times Mira will nervously glance across at all of us—forty-four times—and hope that we are getting along. And I know how many times Ben will look at me when I am looking away—five—wondering just what is wrong with me, because even though my eyes can't see him, I feel the scrutiny of his gaze. And I know all this, with amazingly little effort. After almost two years, their habits have, in an odd sort of way, become mine.

"Look at Isabel," Ben says. "There are 364 other days she could have gotten sick."

I mash my lumps against the side of my bowl. Lumps are not fair either. Not day after day after day.

Isabel is not a friend. I do not have friends at Hedgebrook. But still, I mull over Ben's words.

"Curtis? You're quiet. Nothing to add to the breakfast conversation?" Mrs. Wicket has resumed her multitasking, eating her toast, reading her paper, and making sure no one is left out. Curtis shakes his head. He makes a point to eat with us every day but rarely says anything unless Mrs. Wicket almost forms the words for him.

"And Faith? Where's she?" I ask.

Mrs. Wicket sets her paper down and looks over her reading glasses.

Ben looks at me and then Mrs. Wicket. She sits up straight and stiff. Aidan obviously doesn't catch Mrs. Wicket's body language and blurts out, "She's *with child*. You didn't notice? She's leaving."

It was no secret that Faith was blossoming daily. And we had all had sex ed and knew exactly why.

"But what—"

"We don't gossip here at Hedgebrook," Mrs. Wicket warns.

"Of course we do," Jillian says.

"But not very much," Mira clarifies.

"Why does she have to leave?" I ask.

"We aren't really set up for babies here," Mrs. Wicket says.

"And the boy, does he have to leave too?" I ask.

"He doesn't attend Hedgebrook."

"Well, I bet wherever he attends school, he's not missing a single day of it," Jillian says.

The room dims. I think I am the only one to notice. And then it lightens again, like a cloud has passed the sun. For a brief moment everyone is frozen in time, like the sculptures that decorate the garden, and I look at each one, wondering at how easily their lives are intersected by simple things beyond their control, like wind and clouds and people.

"Aren't you going to ask where Seth is, Des?" Mira asks.

Seth is new this year, and just because I happened to notice him when he first arrived and made a comment about his scruffy blond hair, Mira seems to think I have an interest in him. Which I don't, of course, because that would break my number-one rule: Don't get attached. But I can't stop observing. It is my habit, always on the outside, looking at the armor others clothe themselves with, comparing their natures with my own, trying to imagine how they got that way and understand why circumstances crowd into one life and not another. Seth is connection to my distance, smiles and easiness to my everyday calculations, and I wonder at the divergent paths that have created us. But I don't wonder overly much. I find his smoothness impossibly annoying, and I don't really care where he is, but Mira still watches me, waiting for a response.

"All right, Mira," I sigh. "Where's Seth?"

Aidan steals Mira's wind. "He has early-morning trash duty."

"What did he *do*?" Jillian asks, leaning forward, the scoop about Seth far more interesting than her shriveled sausage.

I see Mrs. Wicket faintly shake her head, resigned to the passing of the story.

Aidan tips his chair back. "Yesterday in English lit, Mr. Bingham opened the window—"

"And a strong breeze flew in!" Mira finishes. "It blew some papers off the desk—"

"And it blew his *hair*."

"Oh, my God, not his—"

"That's right! His comb-over!" Aidan confirms. "The whole class was trying not to laugh and then Seth raised his hand. Mr. Bingham calls on him, and Seth says, 'Uh, Mr. Bingham . . . looks like the lid on your treasure chest is open.'"

Squeals and snorts explode through the dining room. Mrs. Wicket clears her throat.

"What did Bingham do?" Jillian asks.

"*Mr.* Bingham," Mrs. Wicket corrects her.

"What else could he do?" Aidan answers. "He shut the lid. And once the whole class quit laughing, he gave Seth detention and trash duty."

"That hardly seems fair," Jillian says, picking up her sausage with her fingers and nibbling on it.

"It's an English class, after all," Ben reminds everyone. "And Seth did use a metaphor."

"A good one too."

"He really should've gotten extra credit, don't you think?" Mira adds. "It was a compliment of sorts."

"Extra credit is what would have been fair."

"That's right," Curtis adds so that now he has officially been part of the breakfast conversation.

Mrs. Wicket smiles. "Finish up, now. Ten minutes until classes." She gulps down the last of her tea and stands, like she has every morning since I've been here, then claps her hands to send us on our way.

As we gather our dishes, Miss Plunkett enters with a piece of paper. Miss Plunkett is new and doesn't know all the students yet. "This call came a few minutes ago. They said you would inform Miss . . ." she looks at the note again and says, "Miss Faraday?"

I look up from my oatmeal.

Mrs. Wicket briefly scans the note and then looks at me. "Oh, Destiny, dear. There was a phone call. It appears someone has stolen the tires—all four of them—from your aunt Edie's car. She won't be able to come today, but—"

I stand, my chair screeching behind me.

Everyone stops and stares at me like I am a fragile twit. Which I am not.

"Seth's a fool," I say. I snatch up my empty bowl and juice glass. "It would have been much more cruel to remain silent and let Mr. Bingham teach his entire lesson looking like a ridiculous lopsided rooster." I throw my dishes into the dirty dish bin near the door. "And *that* is what would have been entirely fair."

3

I GENERALLY TRY TO STAY OUT of trouble at Hedgebrook, and I am generally successful. But today, I'm afraid, trouble is already mine. I notice on my first step outside that it is a cloudless, windless day, as Mrs. Wicket had predicted. Yes, I can imagine things when I choose to. I can even be happily delusional if it suits me, which it often does. But I am always deadly observant, and I do know the difference between fantasy and fact. Back in the dining room, the sun dimmed on a cloudless day. And that is fact.

Instead of hurrying to my civics course as I should, I walk to the other side of Carroll Hall dormitory in search of a lone cloud, perhaps hiding in the garden because it is a pleasant place to be and because it is October 19, and I don't take coincidences lightly. But once there, I only find myself standing in the middle of an empty garden under a clear blue sky. Not even the tiniest bit of spun sugar clings to a spruce.

I hear the distant sound of the late bell. It echoes through the air in a strange curvy way, like it's trying to find its way to me, to let me know, *Don't hurry, Des—it's too late anyway. You're too late again.* I walk farther down the gravel path to a long stone bench that sits among the well-trimmed hedges and slowly ease myself down, like if I am quiet enough and gentle enough, maybe the world will leave me alone. I feel the emptiness of the garden. No wind. No clouds. No Aunt Edie. The stillness is odd, like the garden is holding its breath, or maybe it is just me who is doing the holding. Four tires, all gone. A sufficient excuse. Aunt Edie will not be coming.

A cold tremble crawls the length of my spine and spins around in my chest, and only because I am completely alone, I allow myself to lean forward and bury my face in my hands. The trembling grows, until it is shaking my throat like a furious switch. I rock, keeping my mouth shut tight. If I keep it tight, I will win. I silently count. *One, two, three . . .*

"Shouldn't you be in class?"

A gasp of air explodes from my throat and I sit up straight. A stranger sits on the other end of the bench.

"Who are you?" he asks.

"None of your business! It's rude to interrupt someone that way!" I clasp my hands between my knees, trying to keep them still. "You startled me," I add.

"Were you crying?"

I narrow my eyes at the stranger. "Are you a serial killer?"

"Mr. Nestor."

"I've never seen you here before."

"A visiting teacher. Calculus."

"Why aren't *you* in class?" I ask.

"And now we're back to where we started, aren't we?"

I study the stranger. He is an odd man. Not odd in his features. Those are mostly plain. Professorish. A thick tuft of hair that needs a comb. A short, trimmed beard with a frosting of white on the edges. A cheap dated suit in need of a good pressing. But the way he speaks, slow and calm, like he has all the time in the world, like he has planned to meet me out here in this garden. And that is impossible since I didn't know I was coming here myself.

"You came out of nowhere. I didn't hear you walk up," I say.

He points to his shoes. Rubber soled. "You didn't answer my question," he says.

"No. I was only stretching. Yoga. Haven't you heard of it?" He is trying my patience and rapidly turning my trembling to agitation.

"Yoga." He draws the word out and rubs his chin, the wiry hairs on his chin bristling like a hemp doormat.

Extreme agitation.

"Yoga," he says again, like there is some deep hidden meaning to it.

"All right, it wasn't yoga! But I *wasn't* crying."

He is not an observant man. I can see that already.

"But you were distressed. What is there to be distressed about on such a beautiful October day?"

I stand. I have no time for dense thinkers. "We're done."

"Have I said something?"

Rude! Forward! Intruding on my space! I don't even know him!

I sit. He's not going to drive me away. Even if he is a teacher. Even if I am late for class. I was here first, and today that matters. *Today.* I will make it matter. I glare, hard and deep, drilling into his eyes, so he can see I am not distressed.

"It's not a beautiful day for everyone, Mr. Nestor. It's not for me."

"Is there something I can do? Something you want?"

Why doesn't he leave me alone?

He raises his eyebrows in the most annoying fashion and then, as if that is not bad enough, he tilts his head! Like I am obligated to tell him!

That's it. That is absolutely it. I stand. I sit. I look away. I look back. The trembling that circled my spine has shot to my mouth like a burst of fire, ignited by this doltish teacher. Counting to three or a hundred won't keep my mouth shut.

"Something I want?" I stand again. *"Something I want?"*

"Yes."

My vision explodes. My hands fly over my head. *"Want?"* I circle around the bench and stop when I am standing inches from his cheap-trousered knees. "You *really* want to know?"

"I don't ask idle questions."

I squeeze my eyes shut and pinch the bridge of my nose. *One, two, three . . .*

"Four tires! I want four matching tires! Is that too much to ask?" He begins to open his mouth, but I stop him. "I'm not done! Not by a mile! I want oatmeal with-out lumps! For one miraculous day, I want Cook to stand there and stir the mush the way it's supposed to be stirred!" I walk three steps away and three back, this time even closer to his face. "I want a bed that will be mine, not just for a month or a year, but for the rest of my life! I want letters from home! I want my parents to know what it's like to be abandoned!"

"Is that—"

"*And I want Seth to get extra credit!*" My knees ache and my throat knots. I sit on the bench and look at him, an unblinking, impossibly long stare. "I'll tell you what I want," I whisper between gritted teeth. "All I want is *one* day where the good guys win. One day where the world makes sense. Just one day, where the world is fair. Where it all adds up to what it should be. *Just one single fair day.* Is that too much to ask? That's what I want."

"A fair day," he says, like he has never heard the words before. He stands, his index finger tapping his lips. "A completely fair day. Interesting." He turns and looks at me. His pale eyes narrow, looking so far into mine, I shiver. "What would that do?" he asks. "How would *one* fair day make a difference to you?"

How? I don't know.

There is no answer for a question like that. It's an endless circling question that feeds on itself over and over again like a snake eating its tail. It can only go so far. I know. I've asked myself that exact question countless times. I look at my lap. My knees bounce, and I press with my hands to steady them. One day. Maybe I would feel less like a pawn in a game. Or maybe it would make me feel that the inequity of the world comes full circle eventually and it all evens out. Maybe it would make me believe again, in what, I'm not sure. Some sense of order. Meaning. Purpose. Maybe it would give me courage to make it through the other days that aren't so fair. Or maybe it would just make me feel like someone is listening. Or . . . maybe it would just plain feel good. All the way through every inch of me, it might feel wonderfully and deliciously good. For one day. Is there anything wrong with that?

"Maybe—" I look up to answer. Mr. Nestor is gone. I stand and twirl around. Gone! My first assessment of him was accurate. A rumpled rude clod! He didn't even wait for me to answer! Calculus! I bend down and grab a handful of gravel. "Go calculate this!" I yell, flinging it as far as I can. The gravel and my words are swallowed up by the empty garden, and the silence returns. I dust off my hand on the front of my uniform.

Wasted emotion. But no one has seen it. I sigh and shake my head. Any remnant of trembling is shaken off. I head back down the garden path. I've missed half of civics by now, all because of a cloudless sky that mattered to no one but me and because of an ill-bred teacher who couldn't be bothered to wait and hear my answer to his stupid question. And it is all my own fault, really, for not sticking with the prescribed routine.

I turn at the end of Carroll Hall, and I see a peculiar sight. Not ten yards from me, parked on the lawn beneath a giant spruce, is a car. I am not familiar with the makes of cars, but it is a very long, barely pink thing with a white leather top that has been folded back, unusual but attractive, something I might choose for myself if I were to have a car. I have never seen it at Hedgebrook before. All the teachers here drive modest, sensible cars, and they certainly never park them on the lawn. The driver's-side door is wide open, and I can hear the engine humming. Who would be so careless? When the headmaster sees this . . .

I walk closer and reach out, running my fingers along the buttery smooth fender. The tires catch my attention. An old-fashioned sort with white on the sides. The two I can see are in pristine condition, like they have never seen the road. I bend down and look at myself in the convex, shiny hubcap, the world behind me distorted, my own image strangely accurate.

I stand. Someone is quite irresponsible to leave it running unattended like this. I turn and walk away, and a thought stops me. It must belong to the rude teacher. He is just the type who would be so irresponsible as to leave a car with the engine running—and on the lawn, of all things! I fume, wondering how someone in his position could be so foolish. I stomp up the steps toward the center quad. It would serve him right if someone just took off with it. It would serve—

I whirl around and look at the car still purring beneath the trees, its four precious tires begging to hit the road. It would serve *me right*. But a technicality as wide as the ocean lies between me and those tires. I am a newly minted seventeen, and I have never had a single driving lesson. My parents haven't provided for that little detail. I don't know how to drive. Not like many of the other students—

Seth! I turn again and run up the steps. I heard Mira say he has his own car back home. He must be able to drive. And right now he is wandering around Hedgebrook picking up trash, probably disgruntled at the injustice of it all. It's time for his break. I am granting it. I stop at the edge of the quad and scan the garden for movement. The only human form is the grotesque statue of Argus Hedgebrook at its center, an art commission gone terribly wrong, and the butt of every school prank. His bronze arm extends out in an arthritic gesture like he is about to fall from his perch, instead of the sweeping welcoming pose that was intended. I sigh. Timing is everything, and Seth is not here, and the gargoyle Argus is of no use to me.

I look to the perimeters of the three other dorms and then over to the headmaster's office. No sign of Seth, trash, or any excuse for a driver. Of course. Why should it be any other way? Today is turning out just as I suspected it would. I shake my head and begin to walk away, but then the tiniest movement catches my eye. Peeking out from the base of Argus's statue is a foot. I look closer. A jiggling foot. The slug! I run across the quad to the other side of the base, drop to my knees, and grab Seth by the shirt.

"I have a car waiting for us. It's break time. Can you drive?"

His eyes are wide and startled, like he has been caught slacking, which he has. "What—"

"I need a driver! Can you drive me? Please!"

He stares at me like I am nuts. "I have trash duty—"

"But you deserved extra credit. And you know it. A short ride—that's all I'm asking for."

His stunned expression fades, and he stands, brushing my hands loose from his shirt, swiping at the wrinkles I have created. Face-to-face, I am surprised at how tall he is. He looks at me and I know he is going to say no but I don't turn away and I don't stop looking because ever since Mira said I noticed him I have made a point not to notice him and for the first time I am noticing that his eyes have a dark ring of brown around a golden iris and I find that infinitely interesting because my eyes are the same color and I think he notices this too at the exact same moment and a chill shivers over me, and like a miracle, he says, "Let's go."

"I'll say this, Des—you sure know how to choose them."

"It chose me."

Seth runs his hand over the hood and along the fender until he is standing at the open driver's-side door. "Just a short ride. Right?"

"Right," I repeat, but I know it is already more than that. It is written in the day and in our eyes. Seth can't control this matter of circumstance any more than I can.

We take a last sweep of the grounds before we slide in. The white leather seats are as buttery as the fenders and Seth makes a gesture of ecstasy with his fist. "Who would guess that trash duty could be this sweet?" He gently closes the door, and I feel the world closing behind us.

My heart pounds in my ears. "Go!" I whisper. "Go!"

Seth steps on the gas and we rev forward, bouncing off the lawn and onto the narrow road that twists through the campus. He stops before we reach Gaspar Hall, where the classroom windows face the road. He looks at me. We both slink down in the seats, and he eases forward slowly like we are pulling up the skirts of the car and tiptoeing.

Students seated near windows turn as we pass, their eyes widening to saucers but their lips remaining sealed in solidarity. Civics. English lit. Jillian and Curtis turning in unison, their jaws dropping. Geometry. Seth lifts a hand and waves to Justin Thomas like we are only strolling across the common. Economics. Physics. Mira. Her eyes grow so wide that her irises look like a tiny dot of ink on a sea of white. She disappears from the window. "Maybe you should go faster," I say.

"We're doing fine. Relax."

I realize I don't really know much about Seth. Like the others, I know his habits at breakfast. I know that he is always late. He works hard to make Mrs. Wicket smile, like it is a clever game for him. He taps his fork on his plate between bites, which drives Aidan to distraction.

But I don't know anything about what is inside of him. I don't know what he likes or hates or fears, and I realize that, for all my observing—of which I am very proud—I don't really know any of my classmates beyond their easily observable habits. A breath catches in my throat.

"Can I come?" Mira has barreled around the corner, and Seth stops the car.

"Shh!" he says.

"Did Miss Boggs see you leave?" I whisper.

"Of course not," Mira says proudly. "She was one copy short for our test today and stepped out in a tizzy to get another. But I'll never be able to slip back in now."

Ancient Miss Boggs prides herself on her organization and is never short anything. Why does she have to break her perfect record today?

"Get in," I sigh. She has already opened the rear door and is sliding into the seat. "But don't say a word," I warn her, holding my fist up. She happily nods and raises two fingers in an oath as she sinks down in the seat to prove she is trustworthy. Another time I might be struck at how she takes life's unexpected turns with such cheer, but right now I am seriously keeping my fist ready.

Seth eases forward. We only have to pass the infirmary and the library before we are at the gate to Hedgebrook and the open road.

"Can we get Aidan?" Mira asks.

Seth and I both whip around, but Seth speaks before I can lash Mira for breaking her oath in less than a minute. "Of course, Mira," he says sweetly. "Why don't you skip into his class and ask his teacher for a pass to ditch all his classes for the day?"

The dawning is slow but visible as her arched expectant eyebrows slowly fall. She sinks lower in the seat. We are just passing the infirmary when a muffled squeal erupts from Mira. "There he is!"

Aidan is approaching the infirmary doors with a bloodied handkerchief pressed to his nose when Mira stands up in the back seat and waves her entire body at him. He stops and stares over the kerchief, and I imagine he thinks his bloody nose is causing him to hallucinate.

"Unbelievable," Seth whispers, hitting the brakes.

"No! Don't stop," I say. "Not him too!" But it is too late. He is already walking toward us, his eyes sweeping our extraordinary pink car. Mira throws open the rear door.

"We're going for a ride. Get in." He does and I am almost not surprised, even though Aidan is an annoying stickler for rules, because maybe today, some things are beyond his control too. He leans back, still pinching his nose.

"Whose car?" he asks.

"Des's," Seth answers. "Don't drip on the seats!"

My car? Did I say that? But I do take note that he is looking out for my upholstery. "Seth, this isn't—" Perhaps now is not the time.

"Isn't what?"

"This isn't . . . the time to be talking. Go!"

4

THE WIND RUFFLES MY HAIR. Surely this will do it. This will end my days at Hedgebrook. It's time. I find that I am . . . thinking too much about others, and that is not a wise thing to do. By the time we return today, the papers will probably already be written up. My parents will be glad for the excuse. I've always been a good girl. *There now, be a good girl, Destiny. Mama's good girl. No more tears. Let me see you smile. Give Mama a nice good-bye.*

There are so many different ways of being good. It's all about perspective.

Seth hoots and swerves onto the shoulder, causing a plume of dust to trail behind us. He slows to a stop. "Sweet car, Des."

"When did you get it?" Mira asks.

"Just today."

"It's against the rules, you know?" Aidan says. "Students aren't allowed to keep cars on campus."

"It's not staying, Aidan, so don't worry about your precious rules," I tell him.

He sits up defensively. "Do I look worried about rules? If I was worried about rules I wouldn't be sitting here right now, would I?"

"Why *are* you here?" Seth asks.

"I needed fresh air."

"Teased about your nose again?" Mira asks with genuine concern because there is nothing covert about Mira.

Aidan glares at her. I am surprised. I thought Aidan was used to being the resident geek. He almost seems like he works hard to live up to it, even wearing a tie with his uniform on Fridays, when it is not required.

"It's stopped bleeding," I say. "You can toss the hanky." He folds it, bloody splotches inward, and tucks it into his pocket.

"Now what?" Seth asks, looking through the steering wheel and checking out the gauges. "Should we go back?"

"Goodness, no!" Mira says, standing up on the rear seat and throwing her hands over her head. We are all startled and turn to look at her. She sheepishly shrugs and sits back down. "Sorry. I mean, no," she whispers.

"She's right," Aidan says. "We all have guaranteed trash duty at this point. We might as well make it worth it. And I need a day off. If I were president, I would make more vacation time mandatory. Do you know that in other countries where vacation time is mandatory, they have higher productivity levels? It's just a matter of—"

"We got it, Pres." I am in no mood for one of Aidan's long lectures. It is enough to know I have another unexpected dissident. Their breakfast manners gave no hint.

"And since I already have trash duty, I may as well do something that I really deserve it for," Seth adds.

"Or it might be more than just trash duty we face. We might all be expelled," I say.

They are silent, until finally Seth begins tapping the horn. "What are you doing?" I ask.

"It's a song. On the road—"

Aidan groans. I shake my head. Mira smiles and slaps the back of our seat. "I just can't wait to get on the road again!"

"It's just a little field trip," Seth says.

"A trip!" Mira chimes in. "We have to give it a name!"

"So we're agreed?" Seth asks.

Being partners in crime, partners in time, partners in a few square feet of space that leaves no room for hiding—it is a risky thing. Far riskier for me than taking a car that isn't mine. I put my finger to an ember when I was eight, unable to resist the pulsing glow. That's what this feels like now, like I am inching close to something dangerous. Far more dangerous than simple expulsion, to which I am accustomed.

They look at me, waiting, and that expectation alone makes my heart squeeze like a fist. If only they knew, there is no chance of this day turning out well. Especially not with me along.

Their gazes remain steady, as though something I could say would make a difference, and it is then that I notice a tiny lightness growing in the center of my chest that is nearly intoxicating, a lightness I haven't felt since my last days at Millbury, and before I can allow myself to think it through, I find myself saying, "Agreed."

5

I WAS STILL AT MILLBURY ACADEMY when Mr. Gardian sent the pictures of Hedgebrook. Mr. Gardian is Mother and Father's secretary and handles the nasty details of their lives. Those nasty details include me.

When I ripped open the envelope and saw the photo on the cover of the brochure, I sat down and clutched my stomach, my fingers kneading my skin. I stared at the pictures. There were rolling green hills. White split-rail fences. A towering redbrick mansion. Tall white columns and shutters painted black. It was the landscape and architecture of home. At least as I remembered it.

I remember holding my breath, my fingers flattening against my chest, because the flutter inside frightened me. I finally breathed out when I realized it was only a stirring where deadness had been. I closed the brochure and tucked it away in a drawer beneath my underwear. I didn't look at it again.

But when Mr. Gardian called later in the week and asked me what I thought of Hedgebrook, I sighed loudly and told him it would do. And as I replaced the phone receiver, the stirring returned, and I was certain that something had broken loose in my chest.

6

MIRA CONSUMES HERSELF with titling our getaway
while the rest of us decide on our destination. The nearest
town is the small village of Hedgebrook, which lies just a
few more miles down the road. Aidan suggests we go see a
movie at the small theater there because it will keep us out
of sight. Seth vetoes that idea. "This is supposed to be
fun," he says. "All the Nubel has are sticky seats and movies
that came out last year."

"How about The Great Escape?" Mira suggests.

"We can't go to Hedgebrook Township at all," I say.
"Not even through it. Constable Horn is always walking
Main Street. He'd see us, and our day would be over
before it began."

Aidan and Seth weigh this factor. The small township

is quite familiar with the Hedgebrook students. There are weekly caravans there on Saturday for movies and shopping, though shopping only consists of Keller's Drugstore, Bainbridge Antiques, and the Minuteman Market, which added an aisle of trinkets to amuse the weekly flood of students from Hedgebrook. The constable has looked every one of us eye to eye at least once and let us know that the long arm of the law is always on guard. His swagger down Main Street is distinct and often imitated by students, even as the constable watches, because, like most of us, he doesn't recognize himself.

"Or MADS Adventure? That's an acronym from the first letters of our names!" Mira says proudly.

"Well, the only way past Hedgebrook is through it," Seth replies.

I shrug. "So we turn around and go the other direction."

"There's nothing in the other direction for a hundred miles!" Aidan complains.

"We can be in Langdon in two hours. And to be precise, it's only seventy-six miles away," I correct him. "Which is an interesting number since—"

"No, you don't!" Aidan says. "I'm not going anywhere if I have to listen to your number mumbo jumbo—"

"What?" Seth interrupts. "I want to hear."

I raise my eyebrows at Aidan in victory and turn back to Seth. "Today is the nineteenth, and seventy-six is exactly divisible by nineteen, four times, and oddly enough, there are four of us."

Seth settles back in his seat, for the first time giving me his full attention. "How'd you figure that out? So fast?"

"No figuring. I just pay attention to these things."

"She finds coincidence in everything," Aidan says. "So here's my 'co-inky-dink.' I figure I own nineteen of those miles, so for my nineteen there won't be any voodoo talk."

"That, on the other hand, is highly predictable from you—not a coincidence. But fair enough," I answer. "We each get our own nineteen miles to rule the—"

Mira claps her hands. "Road Trip! Simple and to the point, don't you think?"

"Fine, Mira," I say, and then over my shoulder, "And by the way, Aidan, the first nineteen miles are *mine*."

Seth looks at me for a moment, a moment longer than he should, then starts the car. I wonder what message he was trying to send, because there was definitely purpose to his sideways glance. Does he thinks I'm as crazy as Aidan does?

I don't obsess about numbers or coincidence. In fact,

math is my poorest subject. And I'm not a savant, if that's what Seth is thinking. It's just that I have vast opportunity to think of such things, and I do. It sustains me. It has since two boarding schools ago. I arrived at Parton Manor when I was twelve. It was in Georgia and was supposed to have a calming effect on me. I had finally started talking after years of refusing to do so, and the things I had to say weren't considered proper parlor talk. What did they expect? But I would learn manners at Parton Manor, everyone was assured. And I suppose I did.

Or maybe that is when I learned that invisibility is a much less tiring way to get through the day. It means not talking too much or, more importantly, too little. Because too little talk frightens people and prompts questions. They're afraid of what goes on in a silent mind.

As maybe they should be.

7

HEADING NORTH, THE HILLS DIP GENTLY. The lightness in my chest grows, and I imagine that the wind streaming through the car is streaming through me as well, blowing away unthinkable things. The October air is unseasonably warm, no hint of frost, though the birch, sweet gum, and maple have already burst into crimson and gold. The world before us is a postcard, and I imagine the story we are writing on it.

"A game!"

I knew the silence wouldn't last. It is not within Mira's power.

"A road trip always has games! What shall we play?"

No one answers, hoping she will tangle herself in her own thoughts for a while longer. But we've all eaten breakfast with Mira enough times to know that silence isn't her strength. She is the one always patting out all the wrinkles between us.

"I know," she says. "An icebreaker!"

"I know everyone here, Mira," Aidan says. "I don't need to break ice."

"But this one is about knowing more! We all need to share one thing about ourselves that no one else knows. I'll go first."

Seth glances at me, doubtful. Of the game or me? I turn, sitting sideways in my seat, and look at Mira. She is concentrating, gazing into the sky, searching for the perfect nugget to share. I hope she makes it a good one, because it will have to count for mine too. I have no intention of sharing anything.

"All right," she says, "but you have to promise not to tell anyone. *Ever.*" Her cheeks tinge pink, and Aidan sits up straighter. He has taken a sudden interest in this game.

"Promise," he says, prompting her.

"Go," Seth adds, looking in the rearview mirror, his curiosity obviously piqued as well.

She takes a deep breath. "On my right foot, two of my toes are webbed."

"You mean like a duck?" Aidan asks.

The pink in Mira's cheeks deepens to scarlet, and I marvel at her need to reveal something so private. Does she think it is like pricking our fingers and rubbing them together so we'll be forever bonded?

"That's amazing," Seth says. His voice is enthusiastic, with no hint of revulsion, and I wonder if he is briefly stepping into Mira's role to smooth out her embarrassment.

"Can we see?" Aidan asks.

Mira gingerly shrugs and pulls off her right shoe and sock. She raises her foot to the back of our seat and spreads her toes. A small flap of milky skin connects her small toe with the next.

Aidan's eyes widen and he seems genuinely impressed. "Excellent swimmer, I bet." His voice is not mocking, but reassuring. Mira smiles and replaces her sock and shoe.

"My secret isn't that amazing," Aidan offers. "But nobody knows it—except for my parents."

I notice Seth ease on the gas; the car coasts, and we all wait for Aidan to continue.

"*Well?*"

"I flunked kindergarten."

Silence reigns until finally, in unison, Seth and Mira both snort with laughter.

"Impossible," Mira says. This secret does border on impossible, knowing King Geek Aidan and his pride in excelling.

"How can anyone flunk kindergarten?" Seth asks. "What? Did you refuse nap time?"

"Or cookies and milk?" Mira adds, giggling.

It is Aidan's turn to squirm, and his ears redden. However brief, it is annoying to watch him flounder like a fish, so I jump in and immediately wonder, even as I speak, if I have been spending too much time with Mira. "I suppose you weren't understood and spent a lot of time in detention."

Aidan's eyebrows shoot up, surprised at my insight. An ounce of observation goes a long way. He leans forward and grabs the back of our seat. "Yes! Except they called it Time Out. I spent most of kindergarten in the corner staring at a growth chart."

Mira's smile disappears and her chin juts out. "That is *so* unfair!"

"Completely!" Aidan yells. "I was just precocious. Curious. I mean, they give you those small blunt scissors so you can learn to use them, right? Buttons can be sewn back on. And finger painting! Why don't they just give you a brush if they only want it lathered on paper?"

Seth hoots. "A kindergarten rebel! Look what lurks beneath the geekage."

"Who would have guessed?" I say.

Mira pats Aidan's shoulder. "Were you horribly scarred, having to repeat?"

Aidan's brows knit together and he nods. "It was rough. I had to switch schools. The kindergarten teacher wouldn't have me again."

Mira sighs dutifully and pauses for a respectful amount of time. "I bet she regrets that decision every day. Just look at you now."

"Yes, just look," I add.

Before Aidan can respond to my brief editorial, Mira claps her hands, ending Aidan's turn at confession. "Your turn! Des or Seth. Go!" Mira plops back in her seat, waiting.

A thunderous roar and flash splits the sky over our heads. Seth slams on the brakes, and we all turn in the direction it headed. A distant boom rumbles across the air.

"What was *that*?"

"An airplane?"

"No! It moved too fast."

"A secret weapon?"

"Right in the direction of Hedgebrook."

"Lightning?"

"Not a cloud in the sky."

A convenient distraction, I decide. Whatever the disturbance may have been, I am grateful for it. Mira bubbles with the possibilities, and Aidan shares his seemingly unlimited knowledge of storm anomalies and positive giants, the grandest of lightning strikes that can fly for miles through a cloudless sky. Seth presses the gas pedal once again, and we resume our road trip, our one-day fist in the air to all that is unjust.

Their voices meld into a cloudy rumble of their own, and I ponder Mira's and Aidan's secrets and imagine the injustice that threads through other lives, injustice that has no face because it is hidden away in a dark, shameful place, hidden for years in hopes of making it untrue. Can anything be hidden that long? But then as Aidan drones on and on, showing off his keen scholarship, I imagine a tired teacher rubbing her temples and pointing to a tiny chair in a corner, hoping for the barest relief, justice and injustice flipping like a pancake.

"What do you think?" Seth asks.

"About?"

"The flash in the sky. The noise. The drive. Me. You pick."

I glance over my shoulder. Aidan and Mira are fully engaged in ball lightning and sonic booms.

"That's quite a span of subjects," I say. "From the lofty to"—I narrow my eyes, taking in his full length—"the mundane."

"I'll make it easy for you. Me and the drive. Why'd you come and get me to drive your new car when you make a point of not noticing me the rest of the time?"

"Oh, she notices you!" Mira drops her conversation with Aidan and zooms in on ours. "On the first day—"

"Shut up, Mira!" I say, a bit too loudly. I roll my eyes, knowing my exuberant command makes me look like I care. I rarely make such mistakes. This is not my element.

"You noticed me?"

"Barely." I look straight ahead, hoping my bored expression will end the questions, but I can see out of the corner of my eye strange gyrations, and I finally turn to look.

Seth flexes his arm and poses, though his biceps do not show through his long-sleeved starched Hedgebrook-issue shirt. He grins. "What did you notice?"

"Your hair needed combing." I keep my voice flat like a dated documentary.

"She called it scruffy."

"Oh. Scruffy," he repeats. I think I hear disappointment in his voice, and I wonder if it is because he wanted me to notice him in a more meaningful way or he just wanted anything significant about him to stand out. His flexed right arm drops and his hand returns to its place on the steering wheel.

Even with the wind rushing over our heads, the car is intolerably silent.

"You know how to drive," I say. "That's why I came and got you. And you deserved justice and so did I. I flipped a pancake, and for a while we were both on the same side."

He nods and I look away, trying to concentrate on a landscape that is a blurred pastel like a Monet painting.

"I noticed you too."

I squint my eyes, trying to make the greens and grays and yellows racing past us sharpen into something recognizable.

"And not your scruffy hair," he adds.

Just when I was starting to feel comfortable with the lightness in my chest, it changes. It grows warm and heavy. Where is Mira now, when I need someone to smooth out the wrinkles? She is infuriatingly silent. I immediately scratch her from my list of potential friends, if I ever were to have one.

I fix my gaze straight ahead and try to dream myself to a world of right answers and feelings, and I wonder about the crumpled calendar page in the bottom of my trash can and if, for today, I could be someone else.

8

"THERE! WHAT'S THAT?"

We lean forward and squint.

"It's just a lodging sign."

"And food!"

"Where there's lodging, there has to be gas. Turn!"

"It's just a one-lane road," Seth complains. "There won't be gas."

"Turn!" we all yell in unison. Brakes squeal as Seth follows orders. The car fishtails, and the back tires hit the dirt shoulder, sending gravel and dust flying into the air, but Seth manages to get all four tires back into the lane.

For all his admiring of the gauges, he hadn't paid attention to the low tank of gas until finally Aidan tapped his shoulder and pointed out that we were nearly running on fumes. I think of careless Mr. Nestor and am not surprised that he is true to form with his fuel tank as well.

The narrow lane is exceptionally hilly. Up and down, up and down, and Seth must slow almost to a crawl in order to avoid bottoming out the long car. He shakes his head. "Gas on this road?"

"What choice do we have?" I say. "Unless you want to push us all the way to Langdon."

"Why didn't you fill up before you planned this little adventure?" he asks.

I resent his accusatory tone. "I didn't plan it. It was spontaneous. The moment just arose." So quickly too. I am just now taking in how each step seemed to spawn the next.

"It was amazing how we all came together, wasn't it? Perfect timing!" Mira says cheerfully.

"A coincidence, maybe?" I say.

Aidan groans.

"*My* nineteen," I remind him. "Any of you ever had Mr. Nestor?"

"Who?"

"Mr. Nestor. The calculus teacher."

"At Hedgebrook? No. Crawford teaches calc," Aidan says.

"He's a visiting teacher. I met him in the garden this morning, and he asked me what I wanted, so I—"

"Why would he ask something strange like that?"

"What the hell is a visiting teacher?"

"Seth! Where did you learn that language?"

"You need to get out more, Mira. *Hell* is not 'language.'"

"Maybe that's his secret."

"Which you still need to tell us."

"You better not let Mrs. Wicket hear you talking—"

"Excuse me?" I say, in a voice loud enough to drown them all out. "May I finish?"

They quiet and Mira leans forward, her lips pursed in concentration.

"Regardless of *why* he asked it, he did. And I told him all I wanted was one fair day. One squared-away, good-guys-win, the-world-adds-up sort of day. Do you think there is such a thing?"

Aidan grunts. "A fair day? Is this a trick question? Because—"

"I think there could be," Mira says. She breathes deeply, looking up into the sky like it holds all the fairness in the world. "Yes. Definitely."

Seth doesn't respond.

"And you?" I prompt.

He opens his mouth and then closes it again. He looks at me and then looks back at the road. The ever-smooth Seth is stumbling with his reply. I find it curious, much more interesting than anything he might actually say. "I don't know if there could be, but—"

"*Stop!*" Mira and I scream at the same time. Seth slams on the brakes, and the car screeches to a halt, rocking back and forth. We stare at the middle of the road. A tiny lamb, as white and fluffy as a marshmallow, stands in the dip of the road, his legs spread wide in an awkward stance. He doesn't move.

"What the—"

Our four heads immediately pivot, searching for more sheep on the hillsides.

"Oh," Mira sighs. "He must be lost."

His little pink nose twitches and my stomach drops. His large black eyes are surrounded by white feathery lashes, and his ears jut forward, the pink veins easily visible. Loose folds of skin hang around his neck, like he is wearing oversized clothes that don't quite fit him yet.

"It's a Cormo," Aidan says.

"It's a lamb, silly!" Mira protests.

"A Cormo *sheep*," he clarifies.

Seth taps the horn.

I leap across the seat and pull his hands away. "*What* are you doing?"

"Trying to get him to move out of the middle of the road?"

"We can't just leave him here," I say, opening my door and stepping out. "He's only a baby. Maybe an orphan."

"Wait! The seats! You know what a sheep will do to these seats?"

I am already an arm's length from the lamb. He doesn't move except to lift his soft black eyes to mine. "Hey, fella." I crouch and hold out my hand. He doesn't startle so I stretch out farther and touch his muzzle. His nose is cold, but his wool is like warm velvet. He pushes his nose up against my palm.

Baaaa.

"Don't worry," I say. "We'll help you find your mama." I stand and scoop my hands around his middle, and I'm surprised when he snuggles right into my arms. I walk back to the car and scoot in, the lamb close against my chest. Aidan and Mira lean over the seat and run their hands over his back. He flinches for just a moment, then relaxes against me again.

Seth keeps his hands on the steering wheel. "His mom and dad are probably watching us lambnap him."

"Nope!" Mira proclaims.

"Doesn't look like it to me either," Aidan says.

"We'll ask in town," I tell him.

Seth puts the car into gear and moves on. "That is, *if* there's a town."

"Lodging sign, remember?"

He glances at the lamb and finally reaches over and briefly touches his leg. "Skinny" is all he says. I nuzzle my face into the lamb's neck, breathing in the earthy wool and pink skin beneath, and wonder how long it will be before Mira wants to name him.

9

THE TOWN OF DRIVBY is clearly marked with a small red sign: POPULATION 344. Our narrow lane wriggles down into a small valley and then forks, looking like it has been cleaved in two by a bunched row of mismatched buildings. Across from them is a patchwork of barns and homes, and tucked somewhere behind them is a towering steeple, which must belong to a church.

"Which way?" Seth asks.

"Right!" Aidan says, just in time because Seth is not slowing for directions. "Left looks like it takes you straight on through."

Seth veers right, and we find ourselves in what must be the heart of Drivby. Three hundred and forty-four seems a generous estimation for this handful of a town. The first building on the cleaved lane is a café, which has several cars out front, including a long black limousine. A motorcycle flanks one side of the limo, and a rusted-out truck is on the other.

Seth's head spins for a second look as we pass. "They must serve some damn good coffee."

"I don't see a gas station," Mira says.

"Told you."

"Over there. What's that?" Across the street, past a row of three houses, is a sign, MECHANIC, and in front of a converted barn are two weathered pumps.

"I've never seen pumps like that," Seth says.

"They're just old. I bet they work." As we get closer, we can see a small sign below the mechanic sign: GASOLINE. And below that, a still smaller sign: FORTUNES.

"I hope that doesn't mean that gas costs a fortune. I only have two dollars in my wallet. That won't get us far. Do any of you have cash?" Seth asks, but looks pointedly at me, like this is all my fault in the first place. Which I suppose it is.

"Not me," Aidan answers. "I didn't know I'd be going anywhere today."

"Me either," Mira says, apologetically. "Des?"

We hear a small bell as Seth pulls up next to the pumps.

He turns the motor off, and I feel them all looking at me. Before I have to respond, a lanky man with grease on his chin appears, all elbows and angles and smiles. "Morning. Fill 'er up?"

Seth looks at me and raises his eyebrows. "Sure," I answer.

The lanky fellow raises his eyebrows to match Seth's and leans one arm on the windshield. "Is that gonna be cash? 'Cause we don't take cards here." He waits. Do we arouse that much suspicion? Maybe it's the lamb in my lap. Perhaps he thinks we're sheep thieves? I don't have a purse to rummage through, and even if I did, there wouldn't be any cash. The lamb kicks his feet, and one hoof nicks the glove box. I hear Seth wince.

I'm thankful for the distraction. I dread telling them we are broke and stuck. "Only a nick," I say, setting the lamb on the seat between us. I rub my fingers across the small gash like I will be able to rub it out—or maybe, if I rub it long enough, it will grant me three wishes. The glove box falls open like it is dropping its jaw. It's filled with bundles of papers, but sitting right on top is a tidy clipped bundle of fresh bills.

My jaw momentarily drops too, but I quickly grab the stack of money and fan it like I knew it was there all along.

They are all one-hundred-dollar bills, and there must be at least twenty of them. Seth whistles like I have just produced the Dead Sea Scrolls. I pull one out and smugly pass it to Seth, who hands it to Lanky Man, who holds it up to the sky like he is looking through it. I hope whomever I have borrowed it from is not a counterfeiter.

"Geez!" Lanky Man says. "Don't have change for this size bill this early in the day. I'll have to run across the street to break it."

"You have a restroom?" Aidan asks.

Lanky Man points in the direction of the café. "Louise at the diner don't mind if I send customers down there. Sometimes they buy." He winks and inserts the gas nozzle into the tank. "Her blueberry bread pudding is something to marvel at, just in case you was wonderin'. Be right back." He runs across the street, the hundred-dollar bill waving in his hand, and disappears inside a post office that is not much wider than the front door. Aidan hops out and heads for the café, and Mira tells us she'll be right back too and is on his heels.

Seth and I share a silent five seconds, which seems like three class periods with Miss Boggs, until finally the lamb breaks our awkward silence. *Baaaa.*

"Maybe he needs to go too." I scoop up the lamb and reach for my door.

"You always carry stacks of hundreds in your glove box?"

I pause without looking back at Seth. "Or maybe he's hungry. I wonder what he eats."

"This really your car?"

I turn to look at Seth, hugging the lamb close to my chest. "I think you know."

"What he eats?"

"It's not mine."

"The lamb?" His fingers tighten around his thighs. I stare at him, my lips drawn tight. How easygoing is Seth, really? I am tempted to find out, to blow away his steady calm and easy smile. But the hour is early, we have miles to go, and though I am tempted, I am not foolish. Besides, I know he'd prefer to hear a duller reply anyway.

"Yes. The lamb. Not mine. Let's see if we can find his mother." I pull on the handle to get out and feel Seth's hand on my arm, stopping me.

"What's your secret?"

I shrug him away and get out. "I have no secrets."

"Everyone has secrets, Destiny."

My bones loosen, like there is slack in every joint. I think it is the first time I have ever heard him use my full name. I didn't even know he knew it. "I didn't see you clamoring to share your secret when Mira asked."

"I was just being polite, letting her and Aidan go first."

Baaaa.

"Precisely," I whisper in the lamb's ear, before I set him down. He scampers over to a chubby tuft of grass growing near the barn. I look back at Seth. "So I can still expect to hear yours?"

"I think I might go use that restroom too," he says. He gets out and stretches like we've already been in the car for hours. "I'll ask at the café if anyone knows about the lamb."

Lanky Man returns before Seth can leave. "Here we go," he says, several bills replacing the one he left with. The pump has shut off, and he makes change for us, handing it to Seth, who hands it to me. A large woman exits the barn. She wears a blue sleeveless housedress that undulates with each step. One of her arms is almost as big as Lanky Man's waist. I think I need to rename him Jack. Her smile reveals a missing front tooth. "This here's my wife, Belle. Her sister tells fortunes 'round back if you're interested."

"Well, what do we have here!" she says, bending over and petting the lamb.

"We found him on the road half a mile back," I tell her. "Do you know of any flocks nearby? We wanted to find his mother."

She scratches her head. "No one raises sheep around here."

"A flock passed by a few days ago," Lanky Man Jack says. "On their way to market, I think. Long gone by now, though."

"To market?" Seth mumbles.

"But he is a nice one." Belle puts her hands around the lamb's tummy like she is measuring him and then stands huffing from the effort. "A little skinny. I could fatten him up pretty quick, though. I'd be happy to take him off your hands." Her smile widens to cavernous proportions.

"No, thanks!" Seth runs to the lamb and picks him up. He tucks him tightly under his arm. "Lucky's coming with us!"

"Lucky?" I say.

"It's a good name," he says defensively.

"It sounds like a dog's name."

"Hey, we're lucky we didn't hit him, right?"

I shrug and roll my eyes. "Okay."

So now we have named the lamb. Or more precisely, *Seth* has named the lamb.

We thank Lanky Man Jack and Belle for the gas. Seth says good-bye, but I don't. I never do, because good-bye sounds like forever and you never know if you might see someone again. No one does. We leave to get Aidan and Mira without saying another word, the lamb and a hastily pulled tuft of grass tucked firmly between us.

Lucky.

I can't help wonder if Seth told me part of his secret without even meaning to.

10

WE SIT IN THE CAR outside the café waiting for Aidan and Mira to emerge. Seth has forgotten about using the restroom and has suddenly become engrossed with the lamb now that he has named him. He strokes Lucky's neck and hand-feeds him a blade of grass at a time.

I resist the urge to pull Lucky away and feed him myself. It is not wise to become attached, and I am afraid that today I have not been wise at all. I feel a momentum stirring. Aidan would dismiss me and this feeling with a disparaging remark, but now he is caught up in the momentum too, whether he likes it or not. Why else would he climb into a car and jeopardize his perfect record at school unless some things are beyond even his control?

Seth is so wrapped up in the lamb he has forgotten me for now, and that suits me fine. But Mira won't forget. When she returns, she will expect me to pay up with my secret. I have plenty, but none that I am willing to share. She should know that by now, just as I should have known this escapade wouldn't go well. That is the trouble with cars and small spaces. People think they must fill them with talk. Maybe that is why Hedgebrook has suited me so well for so long. Meals are brief, gardens and lawns are spacious, and classrooms strict. Even the counseling sessions I must attend are, for the most part, quiet. Some things simply should not be shared with anyone.

Mira wants a secret? I could tell them my real reason for wanting to go to Langdon, but then, that might ruin everything. My parents are in Langdon, and the others may know my parents and I are estranged. I love that word. It sounds warm and exotic, when its meaning is cold and familiar. Even words are not always what they seem.

We have only traveled eleven miles and half an hour from Hedgebrook, but we may as well be halfway around the world. Even if I wanted to go back now, I couldn't. But what about the others? I have sealed my fate. Is it fair for me to seal theirs too? Is it possible for a day to be fair for everyone? Who knew that throwing a single day into a trash can could lead to so much?

"Do you think he needs milk?"

"You'd have to ask Aidan, the Cormo authority, that one. But he seems to be quite happy with the grass. He's young, but he's not a baby."

A baby. *At least give the baby a kiss, Destiny.*

But I couldn't and didn't. He wouldn't be a baby anymore, either. My brother's in Langdon too. The one they kept with them.

"Des?"

I startle. "Oh. Did you say something?"

"Welcome back. I just asked what you think is taking them so long."

"At least a hundred things," I answer, "and they probably all have to do with Mira. You know how she is."

"Let's get them."

We get out of the car, leaving Lucky curled up on the seat counting sheep. Or does he count people? I peek through the café window and see that it's packed. We step inside and look for Aidan and Mira.

"You think Lucky will be okay out in the car?" Seth asks.

"I don't think Belle is going to run down the street and eat him, if that's what you mean."

We spot Mira down a hallway standing between two doors marked with restroom signs. She waves wildly when she sees us, and we make our way around crowded tables. A few of the patrons turn and look at us. Our school uniforms make us look like preppy security guards. "We need to lose these clothes," I whisper to Seth.

"You're Miss Got Bucks. Let's go shopping."

Mira jiggles like she has ants in her pants and waves us close.

"The restroom's right there," Seth tells her. "Why don't you use it?"

"I don't have to go!" she whispers, and points to the men's room. "Aidan's in *there*."

Is Mira finally showing her true neuroses? She lets out a frustrated breath of air. "He's in there with the president! Didn't you hear?"

"What president?" I ask.

"*The* president!"

Seth laughs and leans back against the opposite wall. "You mean as in commander-in-chief president?"

"As in president of the United States?" I ask. "Oh, sure."

"Yes! And his Secret Service agents too!"

"She's lost it," Seth says, putting his arm out to open the restroom door.

"I have not!" Mira insists, grabbing his arm and stopping him. "We found out this is one of the routes he takes on his way to his presidential retreat. He adores the blueberry bread pudding here, so he makes this a pee stop. When blueberries are in season, that is."

The restroom door opens and two men step out, both wearing dark glasses, dark suits, and dark expressions. I hear Seth draw a deep breath. They certainly look like Secret Service.

The door opens again. Aidan steps out, a tight-lipped grin smeared across his face. He leans in close to the equally tight-lipped men and whispers, "He told me to tell you he had some other business to take care of. He might be a while."

"Thanks, son," one of them replies. "It was a pleasure to hear your thoughts."

Aidan nods. "Any time." He swaggers past us and makes his way out the front door. We follow after him like a three-car train, maneuvering around tables, Mira as the caboose, pushing on my back and stepping on my heels. As soon as we burst through the door, Aidan's tight lips disappear and he jumps into the air hooting. *"I peed next to the president of the United States! Side by side! He asked me a question!"*

Mira's and Seth's questions tumble over each other, leaving no room for Aidan to answer.

"How could you pee?"

"What did he ask you?"

"What's he like?"

"Were you nervous?"

"What did you say?"

Aidan's eyes are wide as he speaks, his voice free of its usual reserve as he recounts his moment of glory. "I had no choice. I had to pee. I think the Secret Service guys saw it in my eyes and didn't want an incident that would make the evening news. They let me right on through. It wasn't until I unzipped that I realized who I was next to. He said he was on his vacation, and I remembered he'd been criticized for taking time off and that's when I told him my theory."

"Your theory?"

"Remember? I mentioned it this morning before I was cut off." He shoots me a stiff look. "That vacation time should be mandatory. Six weeks minimum."

"How did he respond to that?" Seth asks.

"He nodded. And then he said, Hm. Just like that. Hm. Seemed like he was really thinking it over. And then he asked me my name. He zipped up, shook my hand, and said, Thank you, Aidan."

Mira grimaces. "Without washing first?"

"Yes. Washing, *then shaking*," Aidan clarifies. "He acted like what I had to say was really important. He listened. He *really* listened. To me. It wasn't just lip service, like I get at school. What I said mattered—at least to him it did."

Seth and Mira are exuberant, asking more questions, Mira giving him a spontaneous hug and then blushing crimson when she realizes what she has done. Aidan turns the attention to me.

"You haven't said anything, Des. What do you think?"

I don't want to spoil his moment, and I know Aidan doesn't like to think of such things, but since he asked, I must tell him. "I was just thinking, what are the chances?"

11

CHANCE WEAVES THROUGH OUR LIVES. For some it is made of a golden thread. Will and Caroline Faraday had seemed destined for happiness. That is what Aunt Edie had told me. Many times. It was like a story she read from a book over and over again. She wanted me to understand and know my parents. To understand her only sister.

They married young, "without two nickels to rub together," as Aunt Edie put it. But they had endless amounts of hope for the future. Will was a pilot, and Caroline was good with numbers, and they began a courier business with a rented plane and an office on the kitchen table of their apartment. They took any and every job they could, and soon they owned the plane, plus two more. From then on, it seemed like everything they touched turned to gold. Within a few years their small courier service had grown into a national, then international shipping business. They ventured out into other businesses, which also prospered. Their company entered the ranks of the Fortune 500 by the time they were both twenty-eight years old. Through it all, they remained best friends and wildly in love. But for all their happiness, they knew they were missing something. They wanted a family. Will was an only child and had always dreamed of a houseful of children. Aunt Edie was much older than her sister, so Caroline grew up as an only child as well and longed for a large family. "When you were born, their happiness seemed complete. The world revolved only around you, Destiny."

I remember those years. I remember them well. Seven years. They are all I have. Because, as Aunt Edie puts it, "It wasn't until your mother became pregnant with Gavin that things began to unravel. One thing just seemed to lead to another."

It was usually about this point in her story that she would begin wiping at her eyes and telling me how sorry she was for everything I had been through. And it was always then that I would ask for one more chance. One more chance to be a good girl. One more chance to make them love me enough to keep me with them—the way they kept Gavin.

I only brought it up for a few visits because it just made Aunt Edie cry more. After that I would remain silent while she talked, and I would think about chance and the order of it, rather than the randomness, and wonder why some chances stacked up to make everything right, and some stacked up to make everything wrong.

12

We finally leave the hilly lane to Drivby behind us, and Seth presses the pedal to the floor to gain some distance on the road. I am well aware that I have only eight miles left to my designated nineteen before I must hand the floor over to Aidan, and I still have a few more things to say. Especially now.

He and Mira are chattering in the back seat. I turn and join their chatter. "Isn't it odd, Aidan, how you just mentioned being president this morning?"

His smile dims. "Yes, I thought of it too."

"I forgot about that," Seth says. "Very weird."

Aidan frowns. "Just say it, Des. Get it out of your system, and let's move on."

Mira says it for me, though much more enthusiastically than I ever could. "That's a freakish coincidence!"

I smile. Some things come so easy. "Nothing much to add," I say.

"But you will," Aidan replies.

When he's right, he's right. "I guess you're just one of those one-in-a-million people who gets an audience with the president and gets to speak his mind on exactly the subject that he had just been raving about."

"I wasn't raving."

"Debatable. But since we're on the subject of presidents and coincidences anyway—do you know about the ones with Kennedy and Lincoln?"

Aidan sighs.

"I want to hear," Seth says, eyeing Aidan in the rearview mirror.

"They were both assassinated," Mira offers.

"Yes, Mira. But there's more. In 1846 Abraham Lincoln was elected to Congress and in 1946, exactly one hundred years later, so was Kennedy! Then in 1860 Lincoln was elected president and a hundred years later in 1960, Kennedy was too."

Seth and Mira both inhale on cue. Aidan says, "Interesting."

"That's just the beginning," I say. "Both were succeeded to office by Southerners named Johnson, and both of those Johnsons were born exactly one hundred years apart."

More gasps and amazement. "Lincoln died on a Friday and so did—"

"Kennedy?" Mira says in disbelief.

"That's right. More?"

Seth and Mira offer a loud, "Yes!" Aidan nods.

"Lincoln was shot while sitting next to his wife in a theater built by John Ford, and Kennedy was shot while sitting next to his wife in a car built by Henry Ford. Oh! And the type of car Kennedy rode in was a Lincoln!"

"Okay! Okay!" Aidan says. "Lots of strange similarities! It's hard to explain."

"Thank you, Aidan." I turn back around in my seat. "That's all I wanted to hear."

"Hard, but not impossible," he adds. "Coincidences happen all the time. And there's the Law of Truly Large Numbers. Ever hear of that?"

I should have known that Aidan, of all people, would bring that up. "I've heard."

"I haven't," Mira says.

Aidan clears his throat. "Given enough time and a large enough sample, any outrageous thing is likely to happen. The odds are actually in favor of it. That's the theory."

"There were only a hundred years and nineteen presidents from Lincoln to Kennedy," I say. "That seems like a pretty small sample to me."

"But overall, throughout all of time—"

"Right. I know. Give a million monkeys . . ."

"Give them what?" Mira asks.

I rub my temples. "Give them five minutes with Aidan and they'll all have migraines."

"I don't know if Aidan getting to pee next to the president was completely random or if some force was at work, but either way, I'm glad it turned out the way it did," Seth says. "He told the president something important."

Mira leans forward so she is nearly speaking right into my ear. "And we're all just once removed from Aidan's claim to fame. That kind of makes us important too."

The momentum. It is there again, in their voices, and I am suddenly ashamed that I didn't just let Aidan have his moment of glory without having to hammer my point home with him. Everyone deserves a day. One day. Seth is right. For Aidan it doesn't matter how or why it happened, only that it did. A kindergarten rebel redeemed. I relinquish the remainder of my nineteen miles. "It was important, Aidan. And also right that you were there to talk to him. However it happened."

He is silent for a moment and then says thanks in a voice that is soft and humble and doesn't sound like Aidan at all. And then, almost to himself, he adds, "Interesting, though, that the number nineteen came up again. Nineteen presidents from Lincoln to Kennedy. Yes. Interesting."

I settle back into my seat, silent. I hadn't even thought of that.

13

As we travel north, the hills even out and the vistas become more expansive. Mira becomes our spotter and points to the groves that are on fire with the golds, reds, and burgundies of autumn. We can see them easily without her help, but her enthusiasm sparks our own, and I find myself looking forward to her outbursts.

Lucky sleeps on the seat between Seth and me. He has finished the grass Seth brought along and taken a chunk out of the middle of the seat as well. I see Seth wince when he notices the hole and exposed foam and then his furtive glance at me to see if I noticed. I cannot feign horror as I should because it is only a car, and not even mine, so when I only shrug, I imagine that Seth chalks it up to my much-rumored miswired brain. Small actions can carry large interpretations.

We make good time, and I estimate we are only another half hour from Langdon. By now we have all missed two classes at Hedgebrook. Four absentee slips have arrived at the dean's office. The infirmary has been checked, as well as our rooms. As a last measure, they are probably sweeping through the library, the dining hall, and behind the old carriage house, where occasional subversives carry on their expellable activities in the old livestock pen. Four missing students may even be cause to call the constable, but Mrs. Wicket will hold off on that as long as possible. She is not one to overreact, though the headmaster is. He is quick to remind all transgressors that there is a long waiting list to get into Hedgebrook and our spots can be filled at a moment's notice. It is comforting to know we are so easily replaceable when so many things are not.

Seth spots a brook running close to the road and pulls over. He says he thinks Lucky may need a drink and that this would also be a good time for Lucky to do his duty before he unloads in the front seat. Not knowing the bathroom habits of lambs, we all agree, but I think it will be interesting to see just how Seth plans to coax Lucky to take care of his business.

Seth and Aidan walk to a nearby meadow with Lucky while Mira and I wait beside the car. I note Seth's long slow strides next to Aidan's rapid calculated ones. They are different in every way, from Seth's unkempt blond hair to Aidan's carefully parted and greased brown hair. Seth sets Lucky down, and even from a distance, I can see Lucky's stubby tail wag like he is enormously excited about the patch of white clover surrounding him. Our little lamb seems to be a gourmet.

Mira leans back against the car and folds her arms. "Don't you think he's handsome?"

"Seth?"

"No! Aidan, of course! He likes me, you know?" She smiles, her gaze following Aidan's steps across the meadow. Mira's affection for him has always been quite apparent. She follows him around like a lost puppy, practically nibbling on his heels like they are liver treats, but I have never seen anything except polite tolerance from Aidan in return.

"Has he told you?" I ask, thinking it might be kinder to bring her back to reality than allow her to embarrass herself further.

"No, silly. Some things you just know."

I feel like I am three feet tall and I have just been soundly patted on the head. Before I can respond, she skips away from the car calling after Aidan, and then a few yards away turns back to me and says, "You really need to pay attention more, Des!" She skitters away, not waiting for my reply, which is already tripping over itself in my head.

Me? The Grand Observer? She is telling *me* to be more observant? Who does she think she's talking to? I stomp forward a few feet and stop. Let her go! Let her embarrass herself with Aidan! It will serve her right.

As soon as she approaches Seth and Aidan, I see a few words exchanged and Seth leaves them, walking back down the path toward me.

He hops over the brook and dumps an armful of clover and grass onto the floor of the car. It seems we have given up all semblance of decorum in the name of Lucky. "Mira said you wanted me?"

I roll my eyes. "I wanted you? That's what she said? Aidan will see right through that one."

"Oh." Seth nods and smiles. "I get it. I thought I saw some sparks."

I shrug. "From Mira, anyway."

"No, from Aidan too."

I turn sharply. "What? Deadpan Aidan? I don't think so!"

"That's right, deadpan Aidan. I noticed he gets all googly-eyed every time he says her name, and he seems to say it a lot. At least three times just now in the meadow."

"You're delusional." I pull on the door handle to get back in. "If there were sparks, *I* would have seen them."

Seth puts his hand out and leans on the door so I can't open it. "Maybe you don't see as much as you think you do."

I let go of the handle, my arms and legs suddenly feeling like they have sprouted extra angles that won't fold properly. Being someone different, even for one day, is unnerving. If I were still at Hedgebrook, following the routine, I wouldn't be in a conversation like this, so close to Seth I could spit on him without trying. Maybe I already have? He has no proper sense of personal space. I shift my weight and fold my arms, being careful not to brush his chest in the process. Why is he so close? A flash of heat swirls in my belly, and my breath shudders as I inhale.

"Maybe," I say.

Seth looks at me for a moment longer without blinking and then drops his hand. He steps away from the car and walks to the edge of the brook, sitting down on a lichen-splotched rock. He rests his hands on his thighs, his knees, and then back to his thighs. It seems my awkwardness is contagious. "Aidan told me about your aunt. Her tires, that is. Bad break."

"Yes, it is."

"Do you mind if I ask . . . what it is about this day? He said it was like you were expecting the news."

I hear the carefulness in Seth's voice. Like I am fragile. I am not. If I were I would have fractured into a thousand pieces long ago. Maybe I have cracked a bit, but then, so has the Parthenon. "I wasn't expecting it. It was just confirmation that some days are destined to go badly."

"Is your aunt in Langdon?" he asks. "Is that why we're going there?"

"No, she's . . . she's in Chatsworth to the south. About six hours. I didn't think I could coax you all that far, not to mention we would have had to pass through Hedgebrook to get there."

He nods. "So there's nothing special about Langdon?"

Does he know something? I walk closer, eyeing another nearby rock, and take a seat there. "No. Why?"

"You knew exactly how many miles away it was. It's an odd thing to know, especially for someone who doesn't drive."

"Langdon's just a town. Like any other. And the closest one for us to have a day out."

"Our fair day," he says, like he is clarifying my words.

"That's right."

"I have to confess," he says. "When you came and got

me this morning, I was fried and thinking of ways to leave Hedgebrook, at least for a little while. Your timing was surprising."

"*Or* a convenient coincidence. You obviously haven't been paying attention."

I hear the tone in my voice, and I see Seth look away. Does he feel like he has just been soundly patted on the head? It wasn't my intention, but it seems to be the result nonetheless. I search for something to say to diminish my last words. It is clear that I am not good at small talk.

"It was more than your scruffy hair," I blurt out.

His gaze darts back toward me. "What?"

He heard me. Why must I repeat it? "It was more than your uncombed hair that I noticed."

"Like?" I hear the caution in his voice.

"On your first day, I noticed how you moved around in a room. Chemistry. The library. The dining hall. Everywhere. The way you talked. There were no strangers for you, even when that's exactly what everyone was."

"And that surprised you?"

"Not surprised. I didn't even know you. It just stood out to me, and I found it curious that on your first day you were comfortable striking up conversations with people you had never met. Anyone and everyone."

"Is that how I looked? Comfortable?" He smiles and shakes his head. "I was nervous. I always am. But I've learned to live with that."

"Live with it? What does that mean?"

He shifts on his rock so he is facing me straight on. "I move a lot because of my father's job. I've lived all over the world, but I've never lived anywhere more than a year, so I can't waste a lot of time trying to get to know people. I have to jump right in; otherwise, I would never make a single friend before it was time for me to move again."

Never more than a year? How is that possible? He has moved more than I have.

"How long will you be at Hedgebrook?" I ask.

He grins. "After today, who knows? But technically I'll be here until I graduate. My parents are in Singapore for my dad's new job, but with college looming, they didn't think my mom should tutor me anymore. I'm ahead in all my subjects, but I need some college prep, and they thought the consistency of a couple of years at the same place would be best for me. Collegewise, that is."

"Do you miss them?"

He stands and wipes his hands on his pants and finally nods. "Yeah."

In all the times I watched Seth at a distance, I never

would have guessed he was nervous. I never would have guessed that he missed anyone. I never would have guessed that he had slept in more beds than me. I never would have guessed that we had anything in common at all.

I see Mira and Aidan approaching and I stand. Seth swings around and sees them too.

They hop the brook, Lucky in Mira's arms, and she sets him on the ground between us. He immediately occupies himself with a golden dandelion.

"Lucky took care of his business!" Mira proudly announces.

"You won't believe this," Aidan says, shaking his head.

"He's brilliant," Mira continues. "I said to him, Lucky, my man, we have places to go and people to see, and you need to stop eating and take care of your business. That's what I said, just like that, and then I pointed at the ground, and right then—"

"He did. He took care of business, all right," Aidan finishes. "I had to jump out of the way."

Mira beams. "What do you think of that!"

I shake my head. "Some people might choose to call it impeccable timing."

"I'd call it *Lucky* timing, Mira," Aidan says.

Mira giggles.

And I don't know if it is the first time it has happened, or if it is simply the first time I have noticed, but yes, there was a definite googly aspect to Aidan's eyes when he said Mira's name.

A gust of wind rustles, and I feel a chill on my neck. "It's time to go," I say, and we all pile into the car. Lucky included.

14

I HAD WANTED A SISTER, but when I found out it was a boy, I was happy soon enough. For a six-year-old, a baby was a baby, and Mother had already told me I could help push the pram. A boy could be paraded just as nicely as a girl. And Father was quick to point out the advantages, that a brother wouldn't borrow my clothes or bother my treasured Madame Alexander dolls. The one thing I didn't have was patience, which is not surprising for a six-year-old.

"Hold your hand still, Destiny. You must be patient," Mother told me. I held my hand on her growing tummy. "Timing is everything. We have to wait for the baby to move." She nudged the side of her belly, perhaps impatient herself. And then I felt it. The swipe of a hand, or a foot, or an elbow, I didn't know, but it was my brother reaching out and touching my fingertips. I was certain. I looked at my mother's eyes. For both of us it was a moment of magic. And timing. Timing is everything.

How was I to know that moment of magic was the beginning of me being edged out of their lives?

15

"DID YOU SEE THAT? Twenty-two miles to Langdon." Mira leans forward for emphasis. "And we still haven't heard *your* secrets."

If nothing else, Mira is persistent. I knew she wouldn't forget. Our morning routine at Hedgebrook is evidence of that, and even as much as I had resisted her intrusion at the beginning, I have to admit, Mira had a way of making me a part of her day.

"Tell yours, Seth," I say.

"I'm driving."

"Come on, Des," Mira pleads.

I sigh and then flip around in my seat to face her. "All right. But no questions. Promise?"

She nods vigorously. Aidan shrugs.

I have something that will satisfy Mira, or it will at least keep her occupied until we reach Langdon and I am no longer confined to the same ten square feet of space. "Ready?"

"*Yes*," Aidan and Seth both say impatiently. Mira is respectfully quiet.

"No one knows this, and you mustn't tell anyone, but I am the last descendant of William Shakespeare."

Mira gasps on cue. This is going to be so easy. I decide I may as well make it worth it.

"That's not all," I add. "His unpublished plays have been secretly handed down from one generation to the next, and now I am in possession of the unpublished sequel to *Romeo and Juliet*." I lean close to Mira. "They both live," I whisper.

"Now wait a minute—"

Mira claps her hands. "I knew it! It was just so unfair the way it ended. This is amazing, Des! What did—"

"Shh! What did I say? No questions!"

She motions like she is pulling a zipper across her mouth. "I promise."

Aidan groans. "Come on, Mira. You pull straight A's in English Lit and you're going to buy that?"

Her brow wrinkles. "Seth? Do you?"

"No comment."

Which of course is not only a comment but an entire rebuttal.

Mira turns back to me. "*Destiny.*"

"It's true, I tell you."

Mira leans back and frowns. "If you don't want to play the game—"

"All right," I say. "I'll share another secret, but only as an act of good faith, mind you."

Mira's smile returns. Again, Aidan shrugs. And though I don't see, I am sure I can sense Seth rolling his eyes. The game is for Mira.

"When I was seven I had to have a heart transplant, but there weren't any available, so they gave me the heart of a baboon."

Seth taps on the horn. "Now *that* I believe."

"To this day, I eat bananas without removing the peel."

In spite of himself, Aidan smiles.

Mira smiles too and shakes her head. "Will you ever tell the truth, Des?"

Will I ever tell the truth?

Will I? I don't know.

I look up and see Seth studying my face. He looks away. "I'll go," he volunteers unexpectedly. What did he see when he looked at me?

"Go," Mira says hurriedly, like she too is eager to forget my baboon heart.

"Okay, it isn't as amazing as a webbed toe, or flunking kindergarten, *or* being related to Shakespeare—I don't have a lot of secrets. But this is something most people don't know about me. I speak four languages and have lived in eleven different countries, some more than once."

Aidan snorts. "That doesn't sound like a secret to me. More like bragging." He reaches over the seat and pats Lucky. "Were your parents on the *lamb*?" he asks, obviously looking for something a little more scandalous.

"Weak, Aidan. And nothing that exciting. Just my dad's job. He gets companies all over the world out of trouble. Once he's bailed them out, we're off to the next crisis."

"Maybe after today he can bail us out," I suggest.

Aidan grunts. "I think that will take a presidential pardon."

"That is so interesting, Seth! How come you've never told anyone?" Mira asks.

"It gets old after a while. I've moved so many times and retold my story to so many people, I start feeling like a parrot."

"Which languages do you speak?" Aidan asks.

"English, French, German, Portuguese, and a little Tagalog."

"Tagalog?"

"That's five!" Mira says.

"Only enough Tagalog that I can find a bathroom. Directional Tagalog, I call it. *Nasaan ang palikuran?*"

They laugh at his nasal tone. "More!"

"Ang Tagalog ko ay mali!" he answers with a twang and pained expression.

"Translation?"

"My Tagalog is *bad.*"

"But better than ours," Aidan says.

I study Seth, thinking of the last two months since he came to Hedgebrook and all the times I observed him from a distance, being careful that Mira didn't catch me, and then all the times at breakfast where I stared down at my oatmeal but listened to every word he exchanged with Mrs. Wicket and how inevitably her voice perked up when she spoke to him because he had a way of drawing her away from her tea and her paper and all the worries of a table of mismatched personalities, and my world of observances had seemed enough to understand him. And now, oddly, with more insights into Seth, I feel less secure in how much I do know.

"I speak it better than nearly everyone in these parts," Seth answers. "Not too many people around here make it to the island of Luzon. So if you're ever looking for a bathroom there, I'm your man."

"Noted," Aidan says.

"Of all the places you've lived, where was your favorite?" I ask.

A smile creases the corners of his eyes. "A little town on the German and Austrian border," he says without hesitation. "Usually we lived in furnished apartments but there we had our first real house. It was great. A real neighborhood. Even a yard."

"How old were you?"

"Nine. And we hadn't been there a week when I brought home a stray dog. I had never had a dog before. My dad said we couldn't keep him because we moved too much, but the stray wouldn't leave. He had adopted me as much as I had him. My dad finally said okay, as long as I understood we would have to find him a new home when we had to leave. I agreed, but when you're nine years old you somehow think that you'll never have to say good-bye."

"And you did."

He nods. "We were there for a full year, the longest we'd

ever been anywhere. I think that made it harder. That dog stuck to me like glue. He even slept with me. Giving him up was . . ." he pauses, letting us fill in the unpleasant blank. "But like my dad explained, the poor dog would be in quarantine more than he would be with me, as often as we moved. So that was my first and last pet. I never wanted another one after that."

"What did you name him?" I ask.

Seth looks at me. He forces a smile and looks back at the road. "Doesn't matter," he answers.

I look at Lucky on the seat between us. No, it wasn't a coincidence that we found him in the road. Or that Seth named him Lucky. It was fair that Seth should find what was lost. But it's October 19, a day no good can ultimately come from, and now I fear we will stumble upon the flock where Lucky belongs and Seth will have to part with him. It will all be my fault that Seth had to go through this again, and even if we don't come upon the flock and we somehow end up back at Hedgebrook, there would never be a place for Lucky, and Seth would have to say good-bye anyway.

I watch Seth staring at the unchanging road. Is he thinking the same thing?

But maybe today could be different. I felt it with the

tearing of the calendar page. I felt it with the passing of a cloud that no one else saw. One fair day. A day that is different. It has been so far. Maybe even a day where I am different. A day where Seth and Mira and Aidan know more about me than they ever observed in my carefully orchestrated distance at Hedgebrook. A day where I am something more real than the last descendant of Shakespeare with the baboon heart.

16

As we approach the outskirts of Langdon, the scattering of houses and clusters of shops hugging the road get closer together. My pulse thumps in my temples. Do I recognize anything? A shop? A house I may have visited so long ago? *Colors*. A tangled patchwork of tinted memories that have percolated for so many years within me surfaces. But I'm not sure if the memories have blended together to become something entirely new. Are they colors that were never really there? Brick red, smoky blue, and silvery gray. So much gray. My hazy memories of Langdon.

A short distance ahead we see a Victorian house as purple as a ripe plum. The lacy trim is hot pink in some places, lime green in others, and sky blue in still others, like the painter couldn't decide on a palette. A large sign out front proudly proclaims, BABS' ANTIQUES, GENTLY USED CLOTHING, AND PEACOCK FARM.

Seth laughs. "Looks like Babs sells everything."

"Why would anyone want a peacock?" Aidan asks.

"You don't suppose they eat them, do you?" Mira says.

"Clothing!" I say. "Let's lose these uniforms before we get to Langdon!"

Seth looks at me, surprised, I suppose, by the loudness of my voice. He slows down and pulls over into the dirt parking lot.

Aidan groans. "Wait a minute. *Used* clothing?"

We are the lone car in the parking lot, and Seth has no sooner put the car in park than a large bird lands on the hood and walks right up the middle to the windshield. He turns his head one way, then the other, staring at us, a bobble of feathers on his head ruffling in the breeze. I hear Mira draw in her breath.

"What do we do?" Seth whispers.

"Is he going to attack?" Aidan asks.

"Look at those claws!" Mira gasps.

The bird's neck is bright iridescent blue, and his stubby backside is tinged with green.

"Where's its tail feathers?" Seth asks.

"I think they've been plucked." I motion to the porch of the house, where baskets are overflowing with the long, single-eyed plumes.

The bird jumps up on the rim of the windshield. *Ya-ooooooof!*

The four of us nearly jump out of our skin and then scramble to get out of the car.

Baaaa!

Lucky is startled from his lamby dreams. Seth reaches back and grabs Lucky, and we run up the steps of the porch. The front door opens.

"Pete! Get off that car! And stop scaring the customers!" a tall rail of a woman screams. She waves her arm and the bird jumps to the ground. She smiles at us. "Don't mind Pete. He gets a chuckle out of watching us featherless folk run. He's harmless. Most of the time."

"Glad we could provide some amusement," Seth says.

"You just wait till the next customer arrives. You'll be amused," she says, nodding her head.

"Are you Babs?" I ask.

"The one and only, thank goodness." She ushers us through the door. "Browse to your heart's content. We have most everything."

"I'll say," Aidan replies, mostly in a hushed tone to himself, as he runs his finger along the dusty keys of an ancient piano just inside the entrance.

Babs flutters off to attend to something behind the counter, and we are left to explore the hulk of a store. She doesn't seem to mind, or even notice, that we have brought a lamb in with us. Perhaps when you have brash peacocks strutting boldly about, a small fluffy lamb is of little consequence. Or maybe Babs simply chooses to see what she wants to see. I can understand the usefulness of that.

The store is a paintbox paradise. The dauber of the outside apparently has had free rein with the interior as well. The floor is an enameled royal blue, and the rest of the woodwork, from window casings to staircases, is a medley of shiny yellows, greens, fuchsias, and purples. It brightens the dingy merchandise that has been cast off by previous owners. Peacock feathers decorate walls, fill baskets, and, in the case of a nearby lampshade, are sometimes turned into other merchandise. Now I know with certainty why Pete is featherless and cranky.

"The clothing's in the back." Mira maneuvers down an aisle, pulling a reluctant Aidan with her. I note that she becomes bolder with him by the minute. Before today I had never seen her touch him, much less take his hand. For Mira, the day is turning out to be very fair indeed. And Aidan, who is normally so prickly about his person, seems to have made an exception for Mira's grabby hands. I am not sure who is the puppy dog and who is the liver treat anymore.

Seth grins, still holding Lucky securely under his arm. "You first," he says, allowing me to walk down the narrow aisle. I feel him close behind me, anticipating my moves, pausing when I pause to look at a stringless ukulele, brushing against my back, no sense of space. I feel the heat of his body, and suddenly it jumps to me and the whole store seems terribly warm. I pause again to look at a weathered ox yoke, and he speaks over my shoulder. "Think it would fit?"

I step back like I am examining it, coming down hard on his foot, a lesson in space and manners. I hear him wince. "I think not," I say. "But it might be your size." I move on, and yet he stays close behind, and when his shoulder brushes against mine, I decide it isn't the end of the world. Space is not everything, and I linger near an antique coatrack and his chest brushes my back and neither of us says a word and neither of us moves until finally Mira squeals.

"Look at this!" she calls.

We move forward again and walk to the racks of clothing. Mira is holding up a gray skirt. "I can't believe it! I've always wanted one of these. And it's *my* size!" She flips it around and I can see a large fluffy white poodle embellished on the front. "And it's only three dollars," she whispers. "It's too good to be true."

I smile and wave the hundred-dollar bill I brought from the glove box. "It's yours." She hoots and turns back to the rack, searching for a blouse.

"That," Seth whispers in my ear. "That's what I noticed."

I look at him, confused. "What—"

He steps close so the others can't hear. "Your smile. That's what I noticed about you. The one you're stingy with. You rarely share it. And after two weeks at Hedgebrook, when I finally saw it, I wondered why. You have a . . . very nice one."

I don't know what to say. "Oh" is the only thing I manage to croak.

"Come on," he says. "Let's look for something before Aidan and Mira get all the good stuff."

I nod. I even allow a smile. A small thing to offer for one who doesn't complain about a crushed foot.

17

"THAT'LL BE TWENTY-FOUR DOLLARS," Babs says.

She bags up the uniforms we have shed as we admire each other's new attire. Mira found a red sweater to go with her poodle skirt, and Aidan wears a blue plaid shirt with pearlescent snaps. Mira keeps calling him partner, and he nods like he's wearing a cowboy hat, which he isn't, and it feels like I have entered an alternate universe just watching the two of them. Maybe I have.

Seth's new clothes, and mine, are less flashy, but still far more flamboyant than our boxy school uniforms. Seth wears blue jeans and a faded long-sleeved green shirt with the sleeves rolled up. I wear black from head to toe, a snug short-sleeved tee paired with a midcalf skirt that has a flowing uneven hem. Mira had complained that I needed something more colorful, but the fussy hem of the skirt was the most flash I could tolerate. Our shoes are still the standard-issue oxfords from Hedgebrook. Shoes, it seems, are one of the few things Babs has in short supply.

I hand her the hundred-dollar bill, and when she takes it from my hand, she pauses, staring at my face.

"It's a real bill," I say.

She tilts her head like she is trying to get a better look at me. "Do I know you?" she asks.

I avert my eyes. "I don't think so," I answer. I don't recognize Babs or her name, but I have my mother's face, right down to my golden irises.

She hands me my change. "Ever take music lessons?" She is still eyeing me carefully. Behind me, Aidan pecks out an off-key tune on the piano. The sound vibrates through me. *Miss Barbara*. That's what she called herself. She was all chatter and cheer and stacks of music sheets. And she always brought me a lemon drop wrapped in flowery paper.

"No," I answer. "No lessons."

Babs shrugs it off. "So many people come through here. I guess a few are bound to look alike." She reaches over to a hook on the wall behind her and fishes off a long blue leash and studded collar. "Here's a little something extra for Fido. No charge." She hands Seth the collar and leash, and he gingerly takes it from her, raising his eyebrows at me.

"Oh! *Fido*," he says, finally connecting that the leash is for Lucky.

Ya-ooooooof!

"Another customer! Pete's better than a bell."

We crowd the window and look out. A large wide-eyed man bounds out of his car and up the steps. Babs is right. We are amused.

And she was also right about the music lessons.

Not for me, but for my mother. I remember sitting on the piano bench as she took lessons. And then I would lay my head in her lap listening to what I thought was the most beautiful music in the world until finally Mother's belly grew too large with the new baby for me to fit. Mother said I would take lessons one day, but that never happened. After that, it was all about my brother. The one they kept. The one still here in Langdon.

When we reach the car, Mira raises her arms to the world and her face to the sky. "We look *fabulous*!" she shouts.

I look at our reds, grays, blues, faded greens, blacks, and lamby whites, my new colors of Langdon, undistorted by time, and they pierce me in a way that hurts and exhilarates all at once, like walking out into blinding sun after a long period in a dark room. For a moment it is difficult to see and my head hurts, and then my focus returns, the colors brilliant. Fabulous. Yes, we are.

Seth looks at me and nods. "You're right, Mira."

My stomach jumps. "Shoes next," I say, feeling the momentum of the day and wanting it all to be true and real.

"Onward!" Mira proclaims.

My heart beats madly. Onward.

I open the door of the car, and I am stopped, reminded that some days are not ordinary in any way and never will be. A long, elegant peacock feather lies across the seat, perfectly placed, perfect in every way.

"Where'd that come from?" Seth asks.

"Not from Pete, that's for sure," Mira answers.

Aidan scans the parking lot. There are no birds. "Maybe the wind caught it and blew it from one of those baskets on the porch."

I note the stillness of the air, and I know the others do too. Especially Aidan.

"Yes," I say. "It must have been the wind."

18

I NEVER HAD DOUBTS about my place in the family. Of course, what six-year-old would? Especially one who never lacked for attention. So it was quite natural that I didn't expect anything to change once the baby came. I even began calling him *my* baby long before he was born because I assumed Mother and Father were bringing him into this world to please me. And I was pleased. I truly was. I never blamed Gavin for my slip off the radar.

Gavin was a healthy baby. Or at least he seemed to be. His face was round and plump, and his lips were rosy and perfect. But it is his fingernails I remember the most. Beautiful, tiny paper-thin nails that were like slivers of cockle shells. He would wrap his little fist around my finger and squeeze, and I found this small silent act even more joyful than pushing him in the pram.

I even used my last wish on him.

I remember my last birthday. At least the last one I shared with Mother. Gavin cried and cried. Mother hurried along our celebrations so she could be with him. Before we blew out the candles on the cake, we held hands and made our silent wishes together. "We can't tell our wishes or they won't come true," Mother had said. I didn't tell. I was a good girl. I didn't tell anyone. But it didn't come true. Maybe it was because we didn't celebrate on the real and true day, but a day early because Mother and Father had to leave on the next with Gavin. He was sick. I didn't understand. My doctor could see me anytime I sniffled, but Gavin had a special doctor who could only see him on this one special day, and they had to fly far away to see him. Gavin didn't look sick at all to me, but that was the story they gave. Convenient.

The next day I scowled and pouted, but it didn't affect Mother and Father's decision to leave me behind on my birthday. They were so focused on Gavin, my displeasure went unnoticed. I was dragged along to the airport only because my babysitter had to drive them. Who could blame me for not wanting to kiss the baby good-bye? But they did. They never forgave me, and I have been punished ever since. Or *forgotten* is a better word. Or perhaps I was destined to be discarded all along. Who knows, maybe by now Gavin has been too, and there is a new amusement in their lives, one who never cries or disobeys. One who is, for the most part, invisible, the way I have tried to be all these years.

I have never made a wish since that birthday. Except for today. A wish for a fair day, and I should know better. Fairness is always trumped by destiny.

19

JUST AHEAD IS THE RUST-STREAKED truss bridge that leads to the heart of Langdon. Of all my memories of Langdon, the musty smell of the river and the *thump thump thump* of the bridge road as I left are the clearest. Through the crisscross of girders a mini skyline emerges. I can already see that Langdon is larger than I remember, or maybe it has just grown in the years I have been away.

Mira claps her hands with excitement. "We're almost there! Last chance, Des. A secret?"

Last chance. Seal the deal. Be part of the game.

After so many years of sitting out, do I even know how to play anymore? Tell. It's only a game. And it's only fair. I speak, hoping to get the words out before the safe and wiser part of me clamps down. "I have a brother. He's here in Langdon. So are my parents."

"I knew it," Seth whispers under his breath.

"What?" Aidan's voice is laced with suspicion like he's been led astray.

Mira leans forward and touches my shoulder. "Truth, Des?" I turn and look at her.

We begin our trek across the bridge, the familiar *thump, thump, thump* beneath us, the shadows of the girders flashing across Mira's face. *Dark, light, dark, light,* like an old film that is skipping. I look at her eyes. At Aidan's.

"Yes. True," I say and wish I could snatch the words back as soon as they are said.

"I thought your parents were in another country, or at least another state," Aidan says. "And that's why—"

Mira elbows him. Here I am, the fragile twit again. I turn and face forward.

"Is that why we really came here?" Seth asks. "Do you want to see them?"

"No!" I say. "Absolutely not."

"But maybe you should go visit," Mira says. "It's been a while, hasn't it? When was the last time you saw them?"

I look at her sharply. A long time ago. Too long. Longer than she could possibly understand. "A year." That seems like a sufficiently long amount of time that is believable.

One that will not make me too much of a freak of nature, which, arguably, is what I am.

"A year!" Mira says in disbelief. Her reaction almost makes me smile. If I had told her the far graver truth, she would have thought me to be a liar.

Aidan falls back against his seat. "I see my family every holiday and plenty of weekends in between too. I can't understand how—"

Another sharp elbow from Mira.

"It's all right, Mira," I say, hoping to put on some scrap of dignity and spare Aidan a bruised rib. "I've gotten used to it. My parents simply don't have room in their lives for me. And I've adjusted my own life accordingly." All the explanations I've silently devised over the years are now coming out with practiced ease. But I feel anything but easy.

"Except for today!" Mira says indignantly. "For this to be a fair day, I think you should see them. Tell them what you think, Des. It's not right!" Her chin juts out farther, and her lips pull tight. "How dare they treat you like that!"

"We're with you, Des." Seth turns his gaze briefly from the road to look at me. "If that's what you want."

I shake my head. "No. It won't change anything."

Aidan leans forward with his hands gripping the front

seat. "I think she's right. In fact, maybe we shouldn't even go into Langdon. What if we run into them? They might notify—"

I cut him off. We must go into Langdon. Today. "They travel a lot. There's no chance of us bumping into them. And today is Mother's birthday. She always travels on her birthday. They spend more time in planes than they do at home." Forever in planes, I think. Going to places they won't let me go. I turn briskly toward Aidan. "And that's why I never see them, *if* you were wondering." I look back at the road. "Isn't that what everyone wonders at Hedgebrook?"

"We don't wonder," Mira says softly. "At least not too much. And we only talk about it a little."

"*Mira*," Aidan whispers.

As if I don't know. I hear the whispers. I notice. Everyone has always talked about it a little. Except me. Except for today, when I have shared a secret that they have all been curious about. Yes, my parents have left me to my own devices. Yes, they have provided for my care, my education, but not given me what I really need. Their time. Their interest. Their presence. I have worked for years to make it all their fault and not mine but have never won myself over, and now in a brief moment of sharing, I have won three over. Maybe they can convince me. Maybe I could believe it is not my fault. Maybe on a day like today, anything is possible.

"But, Des, if today we did run right smack into them, well, on this day, I would know it wasn't a coincidence, and I'd give them a piece of my mind."

Why has Mira taken up my cause? Why has she always taken up my cause? I've never understood that about her. Maybe because I've never tried. Observing and understanding are two different things. One is amusing; the other, risky. I don't even care to understand myself. It's always served me well. But like Mira, I too would give my parents a piece of my mind, that is, if I could. I would scream and yell and rant and shame them, and when I was done, I would beg for forgiveness so that everything could go back to the way it was before. But maybe that is asking too much of any one day.

"Thank you, Des," Mira says softly.

"Thank you?"

"For playing the game. It makes us all a team. We're in this together, no matter what happens. Don't you think?"

Is this the part where she expects us to all raise our hands and clink swords? How does she put these thoughts together? I sigh. Mira wears her heart firmly on her sleeve, and sometimes her grip on reality seems to be more tenuous than mine. But I suppose if she can take up my cause with such passion, I can take up hers with small effort. I raise my hand upward toward the center of the car, and three hands meet it, and Mira squeals with delight, "Watch out, Langdon. Here we come!"

Watch out. Indeed.

20

WELCOME TO LANGDON, POP. 34,019.

"Wowee."

Mira looks up at the skyline. You could almost call the buildings genuine skyscrapers. A cluster of modern high-rises in the downtown area that are eight, ten, twelve stories high are wedged between the older storefronts of Langdon, a main street on the cusp of change. A jackhammer rattles somewhere on the edge of the parking lot where we stand, grating evidence of a town that is eager to move forward.

Nothing is familiar, and I am surprised at the relief that brings. The jackhammer rests, and the other city sounds take its place, medium city sounds because Langdon is only flirting with being a big city. Cars, a horn, the whir of a woman pedaling by on a bicycle, a truck rumbling to a stop, friends greeting each other in front of a café, a man with a white apron sweeping a gutter, a chocolate-colored dog hanging out the window of a passing car, barking. At us!

I look at Seth. "Lucky has an admirer. Did you bring his leash?"

He nods. "You think he'll wear it? I mean, he's not a dog, you know."

"Shhh," I tell him. "Why put doubts in Lucky's head? Life is hard enough when you don't fit in with everyone else. Let's put it on."

Seth sets him between us on the sidewalk, and Lucky strains to get going while I adjust the collar and hook the leash.

"Come on, Lucky," Seth says. "Make us proud."

The sidewalk is wide, so we walk four abreast, Mira and I in the middle, Seth and Aidan on either side of us, and all of us following behind Lucky. He takes to his leash like a veteran at Westminster, and I think of the nursery rhyme and the lamb that followed Mary everywhere, except that we are following Lucky. I notice that Mira and Aidan somehow manage to end up side by side without any discussion of who will walk where and without awkward maneuvering to make it happen. It is almost like they are experienced at this. And of course that leaves Seth and me to walk side by side, and I am definitely not experienced at anything other than walking alone. I feel the irritation of his arm bumping mine whenever Lucky veers to one side.

We pass older storefronts, a dry cleaner's, a real estate office, a notary public, and a fabric store wedged between newer buildings, the anonymous shiny-glass types. I almost wonder if I only imagined that I once lived in Langdon because it is all so unfamiliar.

A breeze stirs, whisks around my ankles, the gauzy uneven hem of my new skirt flapping. For a moment the sunlight changes, freezes time, like I could almost run backward and start the day over again, or maybe my whole life. Would I? Somewhere else besides Langdon? Some-place where I know every avenue, a place where my initials are carved in a tree, a place where I have more memories than a scant few years, a place where someone remembers me and wants me to stay? But just as quickly, the sun is bright again and movement resumes, Seth, Mira, and Aidan none the wiser.

"Look who's coming," Mira says between gritted teeth and a smile.

I hear Aidan draw in his breath. "He swaggers just like Constable Horn."

"There couldn't be two of him, could there?" Seth whispers.

A portly man walks down the middle of the sidewalk toward us, tipping his hat back as he gets closer. As he nears, I can see that his uniform is quite similar to Constable Horn's, and I fear our day in Langdon is over before it begins.

"What do we do?" Aidan whispers.

"Shhh! Act natural."

"Good morning, Constable," I say.

He looks at his watch, like he is trying to decide if it is still morning. "Deputy, miss," he clarifies. "Deputy Barnes." He points at Lucky with a stick that is a dangling extension of his arm. "You can't be walking livestock down a city street."

"Livestock? Oh, you mean *him*?" Seth says. "This is my dog, Lucky. A lot of people make that mistake. But he's a lambadoodle. A new breed."

"Yes!" Mira adds. "A cross between a Lambshire terrier and a poodle."

Baaaa!

"Lucky, stop barking," Aidan admonishes him. "He does that when he wants to play ball. You have a ball?"

The deputy's eyes narrow. He pushes his hat farther back on his head and rubs the side of his face with his free hand. "A lambadoodle," he repeats.

"That's right," I say. "They're all the rage in Paris."

Mira leans closer to the deputy. "Very expensive," she whispers, rolling her eyes. "Ooh-la-la!"

"Thousands," I add. "But you can pet him, if you like."

He is silent, carefully eyeing Lucky. He takes a step to one side and then the other, checking Lucky out from all vantage points. He pinches his chin.

"Just make sure you clean up after your *dog*," he finally says.

"Yes, sir!" Seth and Mira spout at the same time.

The deputy reluctantly reaches out and touches Lucky's head.

Baaaa!

He walks past us, shaking his head. I hear him mumble under his breath, but the only word I catch is *Paris*.

We wait until we are half a block away, walking as straight as wooden soldiers, before any of us say anything. Aidan stiffly turns around and looks behind us. "All clear," he tells us, and we let loose with riotous laughter.

"Never in a million years did I think he would buy that," Aidan says.

"Me either!"

Mira pats Lucky's head. "But Lucky was behaving himself. It's only fair!"

"Great performance, Lucky," Seth says. "You were right, Des. Why put doubts in his head?"

So I am finally right about something. It is good to hear. Especially from Seth. "Let's go get our dog a ball." Kicking one foot out in front of me, I add, "And some shoes that don't remind me we are Hedgebrook escapees."

"Field trip," Aidan says. "It's only an unauthorized field trip."

"Right. A field trip," I answer. No need to put doubts in Aidan's head either.

21

WE WALK IN SEARCH of a shoe store. Mira asks me for the hundredth time if I am sure that I want to spend my money on shoes for the rest of them. I am tempted to tell her it is not my money at all just to quiet her, but then I might have to explain even more, like the car that is not truly mine. I know that might bring the day to a bitter halt. I am not ready for that. "I'm sure, Mira," I tell her. She thanks me for the hundredth time. I want to punch her, but I refrain.

"I could really go for a hot dog," Aidan says.

Seth laughs. "You? What about all those fillers you complain about at Hedgebrook?"

"I'm already going to get chewed up and spit out for our little escapade today. Might as well live dangerously with the time I have left."

"That's you. Danger boy," Mira says, and giggles. But the way she says it, it sounds more like a compliment than a dig, and I wonder if that is how Aidan takes it.

We reach our first cross street, and just around the corner is a street vendor. His large white cart is topped with a red-striped umbrella and is loaded with relishes and mustard and ketchup. And, of course, plenty of hot dogs.

"Aren't you amazingly lucky?" I say.

Aidan nods vigorously. "I smelled them way off. Thought I'd play with your mind."

"Liar," Seth whispers.

Aidan is silent, like he didn't hear Seth.

I smile. I would have accepted, even believed, Aidan's explanation if Seth hadn't commented. I hand Aidan a bill from my pocket. How much have we spent? But I have more than enough to pay back whatever we have borrowed from the glove box—and then some. Mr. Gardian is always timely and generous with my allowances. I credit him for that because it is not something Mother and Father would remember.

"Get one for us all," I tell him.

"And soda too," Seth adds.

"It's not even lunchtime yet," Mira reminds us.

"We're living dangerously, remember?" Seth says.

"Then we really should have dessert first," she replies.

Aidan pays for four hot dogs, and we load them with condiments. I have never eaten with classmates before except across from them at a table at Hedgebrook, where there is predictable space and routine. I watch Aidan. Three pumps of ketchup. One of mustard. Two heaping spoonfuls of relish. He looks at Mira and then back at the onions. He hesitates, then passes on the onions. Mira mimics him from pump to spoonful, to dutifully passing on the offending vegetable. Seth only adds one artistically squiggled line of mustard down the middle. He doesn't hesitate at the onions, adding three spoonfuls.

It is not just the new setting that makes this eating experience different from Hedgebrook. The structure that holds us together is not school but one of our own making. Even the air feels different. I notice every distance between us—or the lack of it. Seth watches me as I follow behind him, decorating my hot dog with a wide line of mustard and ketchup. I am surprised how the aroma of the hot dogs has aroused my appetite to monstrous proportions. My stomach rumbles. "Pardon me," I say, patting my midsection.

"And it's not even lunchtime," Seth says in Mira's warning voice.

I sprinkle on two spoonfuls of onions. That should certainly create some predictable distance. Mira settles herself on a nearby bus bench to eat her prelunch, and we follow her lead. "Tell us another one, Des," she says between mouthfuls.

"Another what?"

"One of those strange stories you have about coincidences."

"What makes you think I have more?"

Aidan sighs. "Oh, you do."

I smile at Mira, long and deliberately so Aidan can experience the full effect. "What kind do you want to—"

"I know one."

I look at Seth in surprise.

"Let's hear it!" Mira says.

"It's a presidential one like Des's. When I was in fifth grade, my mom brought me back to the states to learn a little American history firsthand. We had a personal tour of the Capitol, and I pointed to a huge painting where one man was stepping on another man's foot. The tour guide told us that was John Adams stepping on Thomas Jefferson. It was the artist having a little fun over the long rivalry between the two men, which included seeing who would outlive the other. The rivalry went on for years, each one betting he would live the longest."

"Who won?" Mira asks.

Seth shakes his head. "Neither. They both ended up dying on the very same day."

"Unbelievable!" Mira says.

"Exactly," Aidan mumbles.

"Even weirder, they died July 4, 1826, which was the fifty-year anniversary of their signing of the Declaration of Independence."

"You sure somebody didn't slip them both something? Like an arsenic cocktail? On a special day, of course."

"Aidan!" Mira says.

Aidan shrugs.

"Or maybe out-of-the-ordinary things just do happen, Aidan," I say.

"No cocktails," Seth says, between bites. "The tour guide said it was only a strange coincidence."

Mira takes the last bite of her hot dog and washes it down with a long sip of soda. "One time when I was little, I was playing hopscotch with friends and I threw my marker and the way the chain fell it looked just like my initials. MP—Mira Peach—as neat and plain as day. Would you call that a coincidence? Amazing at least!"

I roll my eyes. Only Mira would compare dying to a child's game. Seth and Aidan chime in with their varied opinions, and I listen to them haggle back and forth and I think that perhaps the most amazing thing of all is that I am sitting on a street corner, eating hot dogs and refusing to allow myself to think of what this day promises, for one day being someone different and trying to control a day that has always controlled me. Turning tables.

Seth's arm rubs up against mine in a deliberate nudge. "What do you think?"

I think his arm is getting a bit too familiar with my arm. I think I have forgotten the dangers of getting too close to others. I think I am taking in every inch of his bare arm and rolled-up sleeve. I think if he nudges me one more time, Mira will begin making faces that might make me do something regrettable to her. "I think I need to walk."

22

THE STREETS OF LANGDON are busy. The true lunch hour has brought more cars onto the streets and more people passing on the sidewalks. We have had to explain our lambadoodle three times to various admirers. I even give the name and number of our lambadoodle breeder to one insistent and fairly annoying woman.

"Whose number is that really?" Mira asks after the woman leaves.

"Headmaster Cox," I tell her.

"The Rule Nazi of Hedgebrook?" Seth says.

"How'd you get his number?" Aidan asks, his voice two octaves higher than normal.

"Numbers are my specialty, remember?"

Seth's smile is sinister. "He didn't even listen to my side

when Bingham sent me to his office. I hope that lady calls early and often."

We laugh and Seth pats Lucky's head. I think he is forgetting that Lucky is not really a dog. We pass an old-fashioned open-air butcher shop in the older part of Langdon. Various meats fill trays in the glass case, and whole animal carcasses hang from hooks.

"Eww." Mira's wrinkled nose and commentary speak for us all. The mystery meat at Hedgebrook suddenly has its advantages. Seth spots the skinned-pink lamb carcasses at the same time I do. He picks Lucky up and tucks him under his arm.

"Don't look, boy," he says.

We pick up our pace. One lamb saved. For that alone the day has served us well.

We talk as we walk about what we should do once we have found shoes. Again, Aidan proposes a movie, but he is voted down. Mira suggests an amusement park and then asks me if there is one in Langdon. "I don't think so, Mira." Seth says he is fine with walking and taking it as it comes. I contemplate what the *it* might be. Besides four missing students at Hedgebrook, there is someone out there who is also missing a car. I hope the *it* does not turn out to be a whole police force hunting us down. I am not worried for myself. Mr. Gardian will take care of it as he always has, and I will find myself off to yet another boarding school, because no matter the infraction, Mother and Father will not be bothered to interrupt their travel plans. Especially not on Mother's birthday. A few phone calls and some fat checks solve problems most agreeably for them. Money is no object, while I am.

"I like Seth's idea," Mira says. "Look at the good things that have already happened when we weren't even trying. The four of us together, games and secrets, finding Lucky, Aidan talking to the president, these great clothes, lunch out of our laps. . . . All we need are new shoes and the day will be perfect!"

"You're easy to please, ma'am," Aidan says in his cowboy accent.

I am saved from having to endure any more googly eyes by a sign with perfect timing: RUPERT'S QUALITY SHOES.

I am not one to worry about fashion. Every school I have ever attended had uniforms for day and strict attire codes for free time. Fashion choice was a freedom I was happy to surrender. Fading into a sea of navy, maroon, and white made everything about who I was easier. But ever since I found this ridiculously fussy black skirt, I have been eager to rid myself of these clunky brown oxfords.

Anything small and black and light will be a welcome change.

Seth reaches for the door at the same time as I do and our hands touch. I quickly pull mine away.

"After you," he says.

We pile through the door to find a busy store. Several other customers browse the displays or are trying on shoes. Three bustling clerks disappear in and out of back rooms with stacks of shoe boxes. Mira and I walk to one side, and Aidan and Seth to the other, where the men's shoes are displayed.

"Wow! We hit the jackpot!" Mira proclaims. There are hundreds of shoes to choose from.

Mira and I wander the aisles picking up boots, sandals, and everything in between, turning them over to check the prices.

"Too much?" Mira asks.

"They're fine, Mira. Just choose the ones you want." Like the money is mine and I really care. Yes, I will have to pony up later, but that won't be a problem. I walk away to another display, where several varieties of flat Mary Janes are offered. I choose two to take back and show the clerk. As soon as I sit down, I pull the laces on my oxfords and kick them off, my toes wiggling with their newfound freedom. I examine one of the display shoes in my hands. It is black suede with a small suede flower at the buckle. I can't see a size, but I slip it on anyway. It fits perfectly. I make a lopsided walk to a mirror and admire it, turning my foot one way and then the other. Nice. I glance up to see Seth watching me, and I look away and return to my seat to wait for a clerk. I look up one more time. Seth is still watching me. He smiles and then, thankfully, is interrupted by a clerk. I look back at the shoe on my foot. This one will do.

From across the store I hear a squeal and I turn to see what the commotion is. Mira is hugging a shoe to her chest, grinning so wide she looks like she has sprouted extra teeth. She runs over to join me, plopping down in the seat vigorously. Before she shows me her coveted choice, she takes the time to admire the Mary Jane still on my foot.

"That is so you!" she says.

Really? I lift my foot and twist my ankle one way and then the other. Maybe it is. If there are none in my size, I will take the display pair. "And what did you find, Mira?"

She thrusts her shoe out in front of us to admire. A red peep-toed platform pump with pleated details around the toe and a lace bow. Very red. Very shiny. Very flamboyant.

Should I say it is so *her*? I think not. And I am really not sure she needs the extra height. But I must say something. "They will go with your sweater."

"That's just what I thought! And my poodle skirt too."

"Right. That too."

"Plus they're on clearance! They're practically giving them away! Here comes the clerk. I hope they have my size." She pulls off both oxfords and stuffs her socks in her bra. "For safekeeping," she explains.

I look at Mira's feet. I hadn't noticed before how large they are.

When the clerk approaches, I pull off the display Mary Jane and hand it to him. "This size fits fine. Do you have another pair?"

He grins. "Most certainly." He turns to Mira and raises his eyebrows. "And you, miss?"

"These!" she says, jumping up and holding the flashy shoe out to him. "Size ten . . . and a half. Wide."

The clerk looks up, his short stature accentuated by Mira's height. The top of his bald head is barely even with her shoulders. His own shoulders pull back, and his eyebrows rise impossibly higher. "Are you sure you wouldn't prefer something more . . . practical? Like your friend?"

"Oh, no. These! They're perfect!"

He clears his throat. "They've been on clearance for quite some time. I don't think—"

"Can you check? Please?"

The clerk's lips pull tight in a polite smile and he nods. He turns on his heel and disappears into a back room. Almost immediately, he returns with two boxes in his hands and Mira squeaks and claps her hands together. He opens my box first and shows me the suede Mary Janes with the dainty flower at each buckle. I take the box from him. I slip them on at once. It is amazing what the right pair of shoes can do. Perfect.

"That will do it," I say.

He turns to Mira and opens her box. Her smile vanishes.

"I think you will find these much more comfortable and . . . *complementary*. They're one of our bestsellers."

And much more expensive, I note, looking at the price on the side of the box. They are a pair of black flat slip-ons with a tiny lace bow. They do indeed seem like a much better match for her feet. I think he has chosen well.

"Did you look for the others?" she asks.

He offers an unconvincing nod.

Mira clouds up.

"Don't be such a baby, Mira," I say. "They're only shoes.

You don't have to turn everything into a big deal. If you don't like the ones he brought, find something else." And then on a second glance at her feet, I add, "These suit you better anyway."

A satisfied smile spreads across the clerk's face. These shoes will certainly result in a much better commission for him.

Mira jumps up and runs from the store.

The clerk and I both look after her in shocked silence. I glance across the store and see Seth watching the whole scene.

It was only a small admonishment. And she *was* being a baby. Practically making a scene over a silly pair of shoes. A ridiculous pair of shoes.

Seth's eyes are steady.

"Excuse me," I tell the clerk. "I'll be right back."

I find Mira sitting on the curb outside the store. Her lashes are wet, and her cheeks flushed. She is aware of my presence but says nothing.

"This spot saved?" I ask, pointing to the curb next to her.

She nods, so I remain standing.

I may as well get it over with. We really have to address

her outburst. "Quite a fuss you made in there over a pair of shoes."

She looks up and glares at me, an expression I have never seen on her before, at least not directed at me. She looks away and remains silent.

"The clerk must think—"

"You don't need to tell me what the clerk thinks. I know what others think of me, Des. Hell, I know what *you* think of me."

"Where'd you learn that kind of language?"

"Company I keep, I guess."

"I don't think anything of you—"

"Don't!" she says, jumping to her feet and staring at me eye to eye. "Just because I'm perky and I tend to smile a lot doesn't mean I'm blind! Or dense!" Her chest is rising and falling in deep breaths, like she is winding up for more. I expect her next words to explode out of her, but instead they come out low and steady and bitter, which is even more frightening. "I know your life has been hell. Maybe *that's* why I try to smile so much around you. Being cheerful doesn't mean there's nobody home, you know. Maybe it just means someone cares and they wish they could balance out all the garbage but they're as helpless as everyone else. Maybe that's *me*, Des. Have you ever thought of that?

Maybe I'm the helpless one. Maybe I'm as afraid as anyone else, and maybe just once I wish someone would back me up for a change." She tilts her head to the side and offers a sarcastic grin. "Back *me* up. Yeah. What a thought that is! Maybe a pretty pair of shoes is shallow and stupid to you, but maybe for a fair day—" She looks away, her jaw rigid but her voice wavering. "Never mind. It's stupid. You'd never understand."

I stand there unable to utter a word. She's right. I never have understood. I never tried. I reach out and touch her arm, but she shrugs me off.

"I'll be okay. Just give me some time." She walks away and stops at the corner. I see her shoulders shake.

"I've never seen Mira that angry."

I turn around. Seth is standing just outside the store door. "Guess today didn't turn out so fair, after all," he says.

I look down at my feet, the Mary Janes not looking so perfect anymore. "No. It did," I say. "I got exactly what I deserved. Mira has never been anything but kind to me, and all I have done is returned that kindness with ridicule."

Seth walks closer to me, looks down the street at Mira and then back at me. "But Mira still hasn't gotten what she deserved. I suppose for it to be really fair, you'd have to make it right. For her, anyway."

How can I make it right? I've already hurt her. She's angry with me. And shoeless.

Shoeless.

I look at Seth and then at Mira still in her bare feet on the corner. "Yes," I say. "I suppose I would."

23

Aidan and Seth are waiting on the sidewalk for us when we exit the store. Aidan peals out a loud, long whistle. Mira strikes a pose. I am still mystified by these two and how just a few hours away from Hedgebrook, their inhibitions have disappeared. Aidan, whistling?

"Nice," Seth says.

"Yes, Mira," I agree. "You were right all along. They are perfect." And they really are. In the space of a few minutes, the shoes look entirely different to me. Maybe because Mira looks entirely different to me. Her perkiness has a layer beneath it I hadn't noticed before. I've heard cafeteria talk that her parents are divorced and she was the center of a long, bitter custody battle. Is that when the smoothing over began? When she didn't want to choose sides because she loved them both? Why didn't I see this before?

"The shoes were there all along," she says. "Just misshelved. Happens all the time with clearance shoes. Isn't that right, Des?"

"Yes," I confirm. "Only misshelved."

She hands Aidan her oxfords, and he drops them in the store bag with our others. "You should have heard Des!"

"We did, Mira. We were in the store too."

"But not close up like me. No sir! Wowee, she gave it to that clerk! You should have seen his eyes."

Mira only heard the words I gave to the clerk. She didn't see the hundred-dollar bill I slipped into his palm. Much better than a commission, and I knew he wouldn't want to be caught in a lie. But for a hundred easy dollars anyone can muster some creative explanations. Besides, I contributed to Mira's humiliation as much as he did. It should cost me something too. My tab of borrowed money is growing.

Mira models her shoes, turning one way, then the other, trying to catch all possible perspectives herself. "He said these were the last pair. Probably set aside for another customer, which is why they weren't where they should be. But he said he was sure no one was coming for them." She shoots me a quick sideways glance. I watch her, smoothing out the wrinkles, the way she does at Hedgebrook, so no one is wrong, everyone is right, so everyone is happy. Forgiving even me. In the space of twenty minutes, she has managed to turn her world around and move on. Shoes or not, she would have done the same. No grudges. No looking back. Or maybe looking back in a way the rest of us can't see.

24

THERE IS SOMETHING TO BE SAID for not looking back, but it has never been my strong suit. I look back every day. Sometimes other people do too.

"Will you be staying, Destiny? Or shall you turn your world upside down once again?" Mrs. Wicket was the first to ever phrase it quite that way. Or perhaps it was the tone of her voice. Or maybe it was just who I was and where I was at that moment in time that made it sound different. *Will you be staying?* Like I was a guest who might check out of a hotel. Like it was my own choice and perhaps the sheets were not quite to my liking.

The incident that brought about this meeting in her office was the trimming of Camille Preston's ponytail. I had asked Camille quite civilly to stop flinging it in my face. True, it had never actually touched me, but it came close. Wasn't the worry of it all enough to justify its departure? And the way Camille carried on. You'd think her golden tresses were actually made of the precious metal. I never saw so many tears over one silly rope of hair. As penance, and to expose her shallow preoccupation with appearances, I chopped my own hair off to within a half inch of my scalp, uneven spikes going every direction. I shoved the black locks into a lace handkerchief and gave it to her as a gift. I thought it might squelch the drama and bring forgiveness, but it only landed me back in Mrs. Wicket's office.

Of course, Mr. Gardian, as usual, had already taken care of the main problem. Camille's parents agreed that a check for next year's tuition was probably sufficient to make the whole nasty affair disappear. And my seat was changed so I no longer sat behind Camille and her distracting hair in civics. But the chopping off of my own hair seemed to distress Mrs. Wicket just as much as the cutting of Camille's.

"And now this." She gestured at my new haircut and shook her head. "I know you've been here for quite a while, but I was hoping this time you might stay longer than your past schools. Look back, Destiny. Is leaving what you really want? Look back."

I already had. I looked back as I do every day of my life. As I always must. But my vista is entirely different than Mrs. Wicket's. I see things that no one else can see.

"Destiny? Are you listening? Will you be staying?"

Again, as though I had a choice. But she didn't know my parents. No one ever has.

"It depends if my parents will let me."

She sighed, knowing this was a useless road to go down. And that was the end of the matter, but before I left, I turned and said, "If it helps, I've retired my scissors. No more haircuts." She smiled and nodded. It was the least I could offer to someone who cared whether I stayed or left.

25

ACROSS THE STREET ON THE NEXT BLOCK, the busyness of Langdon opens up onto a vast green expanse, a city park with towering mature trees and wide winding paths. Part of a lake can be seen through the trees. I listen to the *click click click* of Mira's heels on the sidewalk. What does she mean, she knows my life has been hell? I've never told her anything. She's wrong. It hasn't been hell. It's simply been purgatory. A limbo existence of waiting.

"Great park," Seth says. "Did you come here when you were a kid?"

"Of course," I say, wanting to sound as though at least some portion of my childhood was normal, but in truth, I am not sure I have ever been here at all.

And then I see it. The white split-rail fence that borders

the walking path near the lake. The uneven timbers I climbed as a child. The fence that made me clutch my stomach when Mr. Gardian sent the brochure of Hedge-brook. "Of course," I repeat, not even sure if I have said the words out loud. I cross the street and hear the others following behind me.

"There's cars coming!"

"You can't just walk out into the middle of traffic!"

"What about our real lunch? And Lucky's ball?"

"Just follow her!"

I kick my Mary Janes off as soon as I reach the grass. The blades are as cool and soft as I remember them to be, and I dig in with my toes. I used to come here with my aunt Edie on her brief visits before I was sent away for good. Of course Mr. Gardian accompanied us as well because Aunt Edie was not to be trusted. At least that is what I heard him whisper over the phone to someone— perhaps Mother and Father off on one of their never-ending jaunts. He said Aunt Edie was wild and impulsive and had to be watched constantly. But she always behaved herself as far as I could tell, and her shocking red hair was always tamed into a dutiful bun when she came. Mr. Gardian kept a respectful distance so we could visit but was never too far away. She used to sit on the split-rail fence with me, our balance precarious, and we would pretend about all the places and all the people we might really be. She talked enough for both of us, because I wasn't speaking then, but I listened to every word. I imagined, right along with her, that I was the princess in a tower, the cowgirl on a horse, and the trapeze artist in a circus. And even on my own, I imagined I was Humpty Dumpty, an unsteady egg ready to fall, and no one could put me back together at all. I was clever even then.

Mira spots a fountain, points, and I hear Seth say something, reaching into his pocket and putting coins in her palm. Handing over Lucky's leash. Words to Aidan, something like *Go. Go now.* Other sounds too. A child laughing somewhere far off. And music. And Aunt Edie . . . laughing and telling stories. But not laughing too loudly so that we draw Mr. Gardian's attention.

"Des?"

I look at Seth. We are alone. There are two creases between his brows. Where did those come from? "Want to sit down?" he asks. His words are slow and careful like I am a small child who might not understand.

I look around. "There?" I point to the white split-rail fence that borders the lake.

Seth tests the rail with his hand to make sure it will hold his weight.

"It will hold you," I say. It held Aunt Edie. We sit on the upper rail, each of us holding a post with one hand and our feet braced against the lower rail, facing out to the lake. The breeze blowing across the lake is gentle and slow, and yet it weaves through the branches overhead to make the softest of music, like a hundred fingers plucking the stringed bows of the tree.

"Beautiful here," Seth says.

I shrug. "Think so?"

He shakes his head. "Why do you do that?"

"What?"

"Pretend you don't care. It's all right to care about something, even if it's just the view of a lake. You don't lose points by admitting that you care about something."

I sigh and look away. "It's a pretty view."

"When was the last time you were here?"

"When I was eight. I came here with my aunt."

"It's been a long time, then."

I nod. "Very long."

"Want to talk about it?"

149

I hear the inflection of his voice, the prodding of the word *talk*. He doesn't really mean talk—he means *reveal*. "I am talked out, Seth."

He grunts softly. Like he thinks I won't hear?

I turn to face him. "Every boarding school I've ever been to has had their own resident expert who has wanted to pick my brain apart and talk, but I have never found talking to improve the status of anything."

"To each his own. It helps me. I talk my way into and out of everything."

"Oh, you mean like trash duty? Yes, your talking really helped you out there."

He smiles and nods. "Touché."

We sit looking out at the lake, and an orange butterfly flutters close to me. I reach out and it lands on my finger, its long delicate legs dancing along my knuckle. I watch the fragile beat of its wings, mesmerized. One small careless action, and life as we know it can unravel.

"A girl of many talents. You can even charm butterflies."

"Are you implying I've charmed you?"

"Don't flatter yourself." He fidgets on the rail. "Only semicharmed."

"Here." I reach out my hand, and the butterfly crawls from my finger to his.

"One of a kind," he says, looking at me and not the butterfly.

"Thank God, right?"

He smiles. I look away, and another butterfly flutters near my face, and then another. In seconds, we are enveloped in a flowing stream of butterflies, a river of flapping color all around us. Seth laughs. So do I.

"I think it's migration season. Aidan would probably know—"

"Don't," Seth says. And then, in a much softer voice, "We don't have to explain it."

We are transported, suspended like bits of glass in a spinning kaleidoscope of wings and flashing color, and explaining it becomes as ludicrous as counting the stars, and for that moment I decide Seth is right about something too.

26

THE BOAT KEEPER'S EYES ARE KIND. That is the first thing I notice. So when Seth asks the old man if he has a life preserver for Lucky, his eyes don't roll, but instead a small smile plays behind them and he says, "I'd be happy to keep an eye on the little fella while you're out."

Seth looks at me, and I nod my approval.

"Well, all right. Thanks. You'll keep a close eye on him?"

"We'll be best buddies. Don't worry." He takes the leash from Seth, and then his ticket. I watch him take Mira's and Aidan's tickets too. When I hold mine out for him, he stops, stares at me for the briefest moment, and his pale eyes dart away. He waves me on through without taking my ticket. I feel the cold sensation of fingers walking up the knots of my spine. His eyes are familiar. Does he know me? Or, more important, does he know my parents?

"I have just the boat for you," the boat keeper says. "You have an hour, but I don't pay much attention to clocks. Especially this time of year. We close up for the season at the end of the week. Take however much time is necessary." Seth and I exchange a look at the odd remark. We follow him to the end of the dock. "Enjoy yourselves," he says. "Stay away from the swans, though. They can get nasty if you get too close." And then almost as an afterthought, "Any of you know how to row?"

"I do!" Mira says. Indeed, she is probably the only one among us who has ever rowed a boat, but I have serious doubts about her claims regarding that. When she and Aidan returned from the fountain, they wanted to go for a ride on the lake, pointing to the boat rentals. They had already bought tickets with money left over from the hot dogs. She had also brought along my shoes, pointing out how I had forgotten them on the grass. I slipped them on and fell in love with them all over again. I felt like a foolish twit, not for forgetting them but for liking them so much.

"You all get in, and I'll give you a shove," the boat keeper says. He motions to a red boat with a name lettered in gold on the side, *Courage*. Perhaps with Mira at the helm we will need it.

153

"Can we count on smooth sailing?" Aidan quips.

"No, sir. Only smooth rowing with this little bucket—

and even that will depend on your skipper." The old man winks at Mira.

She giggles and offers an exuberant salute. Aidan steps in the rowboat and offers a hand to Mira. I cringe. I hope Seth doesn't follow suit. A simple boat ride is becoming very complicated. Mira and Aidan settle into the back of the boat, Mira on the rowing seat and Aidan in the next seat facing her. That only leaves one other seat that I presume Seth and I will have to share. A very narrow seat. Seth steps in and turns to face me. He hesitates.

"Sit," I order, hoping to avoid the whole hand-touching scenario. "We need some ballast so I don't go tumbling over the edge."

"Yes, Captain," Seth says, sitting smack in the middle of the seat. Where does he suppose I am to sit? I think I detect a smirk on his face. Mira and Aidan don't offer any help, too amused with each other's company to even notice.

"Scoot over. Unless you want me in your lap."

He smiles. "Not a chance. Too much ballast."

I sit next to him, our arms and thighs touching. Now that it is all settled and behind us, I find the tight quarters much less distressful. I can almost relax against him. It is only out of necessity, after all.

The boat keeper gives the boat a stout shove with the heel of his boot, and Mira confidently lowers one oar and flips the direction of the boat, sending us toward open water. She dips both oars and pulls smoothly. We all register our surprise.

"Where'd you learn to do that?" Seth asks.

"I spend a month every summer with my grandparents. They have a cottage on Lake Wannapu, and Gramps handed over the oars to me when I was twelve." She glances over her shoulder to confirm her direction. "Good thing, because by the time I was fifteen, he couldn't row anymore—his heart, you know? But Gramps still likes to go out, and he won't have anything to do with motors because of the buffleheads. It disturbs them. At least that's what he says. There aren't many at Lake Wannapu. . . ."

I listen to the even rhythm of the oars slicing through the water, the barely perceptible whoosh of Seth's shirt rustling against my shoulder, the rattling of Mira's endless explanation of Lake Wannapu and the buffleheads, the huffs and grunts of her propelling us across the lake, and I wonder at where I am and who I am and what I have missed because I have been afraid for so long of moments just like this, places of touching and speaking and letting others in, and even now I'm afraid, but I'm in a new place, a place where I can't go back, a place I am being sucked to against my will, a place where a soft underside is exposed.

That's what today had done. And I don't know if it will be the end of me or the beginning. Or maybe the end of us all. It's possible. It's happened before. *You don't lose points by admitting that you care about something.* But it's not points I am afraid of losing.

I allow my weight to lean slightly to the left, like the boat is jostling me. I feel Seth's bones, his elbow, his warmth, the tightness of arm pressing against arm, the squeezing away of the space between us.

As we skim across the water, the swans the boat keeper warned us about join us, following along on either side like sentries. They are black, as dark as midnight, menacing in their color and stature, but not in their demeanor. They float like black angels, watching the waters ahead, their presence casting a silent spell over us.

Finally Seth whispers, breaking the silence. "The boat keeper was wrong. They seem to like us."

Aidan grunts. "Today, anyway. Why am I not surprised?"

"That was my thought exactly, Aidan," I say. "It is a rare and frightening day that you and I think alike."

"Agreed."

"It's an extraordinary day," Mira says. "And every now and then, one of those is bound to come along."

I'm afraid Mira may be closer to the truth than she knows.

"You're an accomplished rower, Mira," I say, hoping to shift the conversation.

"Thanks, Des. I'll be sure and tell Gramps you said so next time I see him. He takes pride in things like that." She stops rowing, and the swans disperse, their mission apparently complete. We're in the middle of the lake. "Should we float here for a while?"

It is agreed, and Aidan turns in his seat so he is facing me and Seth. Mira boldly stands to join him on his seat. Though her rowing may be accomplished, her grace in flashy platform pumps in a rocking boat is lacking, and she nearly topples over the side. Aidan grabs her just in time by the largest body part within reach—her backside—and pulls her to their seat. He flushes crimson and thrusts his hands into his lap.

"Sorry," he says.

Mira hoots. "Sorry? You saved my life! And my new skirt and shoes! Imagine what the lake would have done to them! Grab away, Cowboy!" She smooths her skirt so the poodle isn't creased and then kisses his cheek. "Thank you!" The rosy hue on Aidan's cheeks spreads to his ears.

Yes, another realm. That is the only place I can be. The

Mira I knew yesterday would never do such a thing, but maybe today we are all in a different place from where and who we were a day ago. Certainly the Destiny they all think they know would never join them in an excursion like this. I wonder about the structure of Hedgebrook, and the structure we have all built into our lives, some of our own making, some thrust on us—girders, timbers, nails, wire—sometimes desperate pieces of string that hold us up but at the same time keep us from being anything other than what we have always been.

Aidan and Mira slide to the floor of the boat, pulling their seat cushions with them, and lean back against the seat, their knees bunched up together. "A game," Mira says. "Time for another game."

No one protests. Mira has earned this one. "A truth-or-dare game. Each person has to answer a question—any question the rest of us choose—or take a dare. I'll go first." I briefly glance at Seth and then turn my gaze to Mira. We lock eyes, and I feel my stomach floating somewhere beneath my ribs. Not me. *Not me.* She looks away, and I feel breath return to my chest. "Seth," she says. "What made you do it? Why'd you tell Mr. Bingham about his comb-over calamity? You could have just kept your mouth shut and let him parade around with it all cockeyed for the whole class hour. Why'd you bail him out? All you got was grief from it."

An easy one. I would have posed something much tougher.

Seth leans forward, his hands clasped between his knees like he is thinking. He finally smiles at Mira and shakes his head. "Honestly, Mira, it was just a big miscalculation on my part. I had seen him look in his desk drawer at the beginning and end of every class period since the first day of school, so I got curious. Finally, one day I snuck a look. You know what's in there? A mirror. He's checking to make sure everything is in place. I guess those carefully sprayed strands mean a lot to him. I mean, let's face it, Bingham is flat-out at the bottom of my list of favorite teachers, but—" Seth shrugs and looks up. "This goes no farther than this boat, right?"

Aidan, Mira, and I nod in unison.

"Okay. The truth is, well, I felt sorry for him. His hair is the most important thing in his life, and I was squirming just watching him walk around with it straight up in the air like—"

"A rooster?"

"Exactly. After two minutes, I couldn't stand it anymore and my hand just went up before I could even think what I was going to say. That's where I went wrong. When he called on me, I had to say something. I tried to make light of it, thinking that would make it easier on him, but I didn't calculate on the fact that everyone else in the class has Bingham at the bottom of their list too. They were waiting for a chance to laugh at his expense. And they all did."

Aidan sighs. "Boy, did they. Me included."

Mira grimaces. "Sorry. Me too."

"But you only told him the truth in the kindest way that you could," I say.

"Sometimes people don't want to hear the truth, no matter how you say it. They want to stay in their fantasy worlds."

Yes, I suppose they do. And until today, I would have seen nothing wrong with that.

"So that's my truth. You can't tell anyone. I had a momentary soft spot for Bingham. It won't happen again."

"Our lips are sealed," Mira says.

Seth slides to the bottom of the boat too. "Better ballast," he explains, looking up at me. "Plus, we can lean back." He gives the hem of my skirt a tug and raises his eyebrows. I guess he expects me to join his efforts at being better ballast. It is not like we are on a stormy sea, but I slide to the floor anyway. He's right. It is more comfortable. It is warmer too, with more protection from the brisk breeze that is picking up across the lake. My whole left side is snug against Seth, and I try to move over, but it is no use because the curve of the bottom pushes me toward him. He will simply have to endure my close proximity since it was his idea.

"Who's next?" Seth asks.

Aidan looks at me and smiles. His eyes narrow. "I have a question for—"

"Wait!" I say. "Shouldn't we know what the dare is before we answer questions?"

Mira nods. "You're right, Des. That's the rules of the game." She looks around our small quarters. There is not much one can do for a dare. "How about if someone refuses to answer they have to swim to shore?"

"Are you crazy, Mira?" Aidan protests. "That water has to be fifty degrees."

I give Aidan the same menacing stare he gave me a moment ago. "It's not a problem if you answer your question, *Cowboy*." Perhaps now he will choose his question more wisely. He seems to get my drift and is not so eager to ask a question at all anymore.

"That's right," Mira says. "Just pony up, Cowboy. If it was easy, it wouldn't be called a dare."

Sometimes I am envious of Mira's perky replies. They pack a punch but are so cheerful and genuine one can't protest. Aidan is quiet.

"What was your question, Aidan?" I prompt.

He sighs and looks upward. I know he has reevaluated and is cautiously considering his query. Very wise because I had a question ready that would have sent him swimming to shore. Nothing comes between Aidan and his test scores. "All right, Des. What's your favorite color?"

"What?" Seth protests. "What kind of dumb question is that?"

"A perfectly good question," I say, and then, looking at Aidan, I add, "and a very *wise* one."

Mira chimes in with Seth. "No fair. I already know. Pink."

"It is not pink!" I say.

"Is too. I've seen all your stationery that you write your letters to your aunt Edie on, and it's all pink. I heard a long time ago that whatever you choose for your stationery is your true favorite color because it's where you pour your heart out."

"That is the most foolish thing I've ever heard!" I tell her.

"I'd bet it's black."

"Do you pour your heart out?" Seth asks.

Instantly they are all silent and looking at me.

"You can't ask me another question," I tell him.

"Aidan's demoted to the lower decks. His question didn't count. Besides, Mira answered it."

"I can't help that—"

"Destiny, it's a simple question. Much easier than mine. Do you pour your heart out to your aunt Edie?"

They are looking at me like they are wondering if I have a heart at all. Or perhaps just a baboon one, after all. Maybe that's exactly what I have. I look down at my lap. "I write things. Things I wish— Things that—" I look up at Seth. "But I've never mailed the letters. They're all in a box in the bottom of my dresser."

The wind blows over our heads. The boat rocks. They are silent.

"And Mira's right," I say. "It is pink."

"Why write letters if you're not going to mail them? Isn't that a huge waste of time?" Aidan asks. Mira glances sideways at him and frowns.

"It's all right, Mira. It's a logical question," I say. "Because the writing of them was enough. The words are there. They've been said, if only on paper. That's enough."

"Is it?" Seth asks.

I look at him. I thought it was enough. At least all that I could expect. My rants. My accusations. My pleas. My apologies. Eloquently penned on pink stationery and hidden away. But of course it wasn't enough, which is why there was always another letter. And another. An impotent one-way conversation.

"Maybe not," I answer. "But there's not much I can do about that."

Seth grins, a slow, wicked upward turn of the corners of his mouth. "If you say so," he answers. He shakes his head and looks back at the others. "Pink. I wouldn't have guessed. Good question after all, Aidan. You're allowed back on the upper decks."

If you say so?

So many people in life think you have choices. Like Mrs. Wicket wondering if I will stay. Sometimes the choices are taken away from you. *If I say so?* I only say what is.

Seth is already moving along in the game, asking Aidan a question, then Mira, all of them moving forward when I am still three steps behind, out of step as I have always been. I have never told anyone before about the unmailed letters—not counselors, not Mr. Gardian, not even Aunt Edie. It is like Seth says, sometimes people don't want to hear the truth. Sometimes a fantasy world is easier. Not only easier. Wiser.

I think about the letters I wrote, the pink stationery that Mr. Gardian always kept me well supplied with, the very same kind Mother bought me when I was five and just learning to write. The pages I crafted over and over again, counting each letter, thinking just the right amount might make a difference. There was the year they all had to be a strong solid number, exactly one hundred words long, and the following year, when I was sure that each sentence needed nineteen words, and then again when each letter needed four paragraphs, one for each person in our family, or what should have been a family. I thought that if all the timing of the writing and the reading were just right, it might undo all the timing of the past. And then finally, in the last year, just the same word over and over again filling both sides of the paper. Never mailed. Always neatly tucked away, because if my secret missives were to bring about any change, it wouldn't happen via postal delivery. Tucked away because I knew I had no choice or voice, and no words, no matter how carefully arranged, could ever change anything. Tucked away because, really, I wasn't sure I deserved to be heard.

If I say so?

I look at Seth, still trading in details and technicalities with Aidan. Still listening, spouting, engaged. Moving forward. Moving on without me. Leaving me behind. I clear my throat. "I *do* say so."

Seth stops midsentence and looks at me. "What?"

"Today. Now. I want to go."

"Go where?"

"May I finish what I was saying?" Aidan grumbles.

"Shhh!" Seth and Mira both tell him.

"I'll row," Mira says cheerfully, lifting herself back up to the seat. "Where do you want to go, Des? The other side of the lake?"

"My house. I want to go see my parents. I have things to say."

Seth nods.

Aidan's brows rise.

Mira grins.

"It's about time," she says. "Let's go."

27

IT'S ABOUT TIME. All about time. Could it have been different? We all know the past cannot be relived, but how many of us really have the will not to visit that realm? A world where you imagine the steps that might have been placed in a different order, a word spoken louder or not, a breath that might have been exhaled a heartbeat faster. A split second that fractures into endless other possibilities. If only I had been a different person. Or they had. Even for a few minutes. Could I have been kinder? Could they? Would one step have added up to a thousand different ones?

I look back every day. The sky was filled with fat, fluffy clouds, the kind that move from one shape to another. A bird. An elephant. A rabbit. Shapes that make the sky look like a child's party plate. A birthday party plate. How could they not see that? A brief spatter of rain pelted us as we ran to the car.

Father was nervous on the way to the airport. He preferred to be the pilot and not the passenger, but a last-minute change in their appointment time made it impossible to fly his own jet. The flight plan couldn't be cleared in time for the destination airport. Of course, at seven years old, I knew nothing of flight plans or changed appointments—Aunt Edie related these details later—but I do remember Father twisting the band of his watch, and checking the time over and over again. He sat in the front seat with Esme, the babysitter, who was driving. Mother, Gavin, and I sat in the back. He turned often to check on Gavin and then would give a cursory glance to me. He lingered once, trying to get me to smile. I turned away and looked out the window. It was my birthday, after all. Mother was too preoccupied with Gavin to notice Father's nervousness or my silence. Gavin was smiling and cooing and not looking sick at all. "That's my good boy," Mother said over and over again, not even trying anymore to play up the sick story. It was clear her allegiance had already shifted.

Langdon Airport is small—only two gates—with one

public waiting area. Esme parked the car, and we went in to see them off. She pulled me close and whispered in my ear, "Don't sulk. Say good-bye. I'll buy you an ice cream on the way home." If only she had known me better. The world had been at my fingertips. A single ice cream cone was hardly a fair trade.

At the last minute, when I realized my sulking wasn't going to stop them, I cried. I created an embarrassing scene that made them stop. Mother knelt and began to cry too and explained to me all over again why they had to go today. But they were still going. She wiped my tears with her fingers. "There now, be a good girl, Destiny. Mama's good girl. No more tears. Let me see you smile. Give Mama a nice good-bye."

I wasn't a good girl. I didn't smile. I didn't say good-bye. I was silent, stunned that they really were leaving me.

"We have to go, Caroline. Everyone's boarded. They're holding the flight for us. She'll be fine." Father gave my forehead a rushed kiss. Mother did too. It was a fitting scene for Esme and anyone else who might be watching. Their final obligation was fulfilled, they were rid of me. They walked away, Gavin still smiling at me from his car seat as it swung from Father's hand. The babysitter grabbed my hand to go, but I pulled away. I ran to the window to watch them walk across the tarmac and up the stairs of the waiting plane. Within seconds, the stairs were pulled away, the blocks behind the wheels pulled, and they were moving, taxiing out to the runway. The puffy clouds above had pulled together in a thick, dark blanket.

Was it too late? Would they know? I began to lift my hand. Maybe they would look out the window and see me. But the timing. Changed appointments. Changed planes. Running late. A hundred unrelated events that choose to come together at a single moment. A weaving of errors that some might call coincidence. I was too late. My face flushed hot. They were gone. They didn't look back. They left without me. "Destiny!" The babysitter pulled me away from the window. She pressed my face into her belly. She pressed so tight I couldn't breathe. Or maybe I stopped on my own. They left me. My parents and Gavin left me behind.

If that wasn't enough, they sent me away when they returned, out of the house so I wouldn't taint their good little boy. Moving on without me. Not that I care anymore. It's been too long to care.

28

IT IS DECIDED THAT WE WILL "finish our escapades" in Langdon, as Mira put it, before we go to my house, which is beyond the outskirts of town. That way, as I explained, if things turn sour, we will at least have our day in Langdon to remember—and as I didn't explain, I will still have time to change my mind. When we return with our boat, we see all the other boats battened down for the winter, pulled onto scaffolds on the shore, canvas stretched tight over their tops.

"I thought he wasn't closing up until the end of the week."

"Changed his mind, I guess."

"The weather is turning."

"But how did he get all those boats put up so fast?"

"He's too old."

"Must have had help."

We see the boat keeper at the end of the dock waving us in, Lucky by his side. Mira expertly guides us close to the dock, and the boat keeper slips a rope over the cleat to secure us.

Baaaa.

"Miss us, fella?" Seth says, unmistakably relieved that the boat keeper didn't abscond with Lucky.

We get out of the boat, saying our hellos to Lucky, who is happy to see us. "Look, his tail is wagging."

"Do you think it means the same thing as a dog's wagging tail?"

"Of course it does!"

"I don't think so, Mira."

Baaaa.

Seth picks him up. "Let's go get him a snack. Thanks for—" He turns around, looking in all directions. "Where'd he go?" We turn too. The boat keeper is gone. Off the dock. Out of sight.

"When he closes up, he doesn't waste time, does he?"

Apparently not. I scan the shore, the park, the shadows in the trees beyond. He is gone.

"He probably wanted to get lunch."

"At three o'clock?"

"Sounds good to me."

We indulge Aidan. Our first stop is our second lunch of the day. This time pizza by the slice. I get three. Pepperoni. Hawaiian. Veggie.

The money flows.

We have our picture taken at a novelty studio, Seth and Aidan as gunslingers and Mira and I as saloon girls.

We get henna tattoos; mine is a thorny vine that wraps around my upper arm like a piece of jewelry.

We shoot cardboard ducks at the arcade.

Minutes later, we are saving a mama duck and her brood of four ducklings who are crossing a busy road. Aidan notes the irony. Mira notes the fairness. Seth notes the timing. I try to note nothing at all.

The afternoon is giddy. Lightness. I only allow myself to think of what comes next. Not later. Minutes, seconds, in the moment, in the now. It's like it is all happening in one long inhaled breath. Keep moving, don't think. I am smiling. One time I laugh. A loud belly laugh. It draws looks from the others. I don't blame them. It sounds foreign to me too. Aidan even whispers under his breath to Mira, *What's with her?*

A fair day. That's what. For a couple of hours, I am out-running chance. It is a day like no other. A once-in-a-lifetime day, and it makes me wonder: What kind of journey am I really on? One to lead me away from all that is unfair in my life, or a journey to lead me back to all that is right?

We pass an appliance store. A dozen televisions all on the same channel fill the front window—a travel channel showing the green hills of Austria. I am hoping Mira doesn't break out in song. A salesman within walks to the door and opens it like he's been expecting us. Suddenly the green hills disappear from the televisions and are replaced with a News Alert message. Seconds later, the president appears at a podium. Aidan is already walking through the open door of the store, and we are right behind him to hear what the news is about.

"He's still wearing the same clothes from this morning! I saw that shirt. I almost touched that shirt!"

"Shhh!"

The voice of an unseen reporter tells us that the president is holding an impromptu press conference from his mountain weekend retreat. He called for the conference to announce something important. The president smiles and begins.

"Thank you all for coming on such short notice. I've been thinking about and discussing this for a long time with my advisers, but just this morning I spoke with a young man . . ."

The president goes on to describe a patriotic teen that he met in a small town not far from his retreat, a boy that any of us might know, he could be our brother, our son, our student, a bright young man with hopes and dreams for the future of our great county. I wanted to reach inside the television and shake the president and tell him to stop. Now Aidan would be insufferable for at least the next decade.

"But I can't think of a more fitting place to make this announcement than here in the mountains among the pines and birches, where countless Americans have trekked to refresh their souls and minds. And so I am asking Congress to form a committee—"

Mira claps her hands. "You, Aidan! He was talking about you!"

"Shhh!"

"The cost and negative effects of worker burnout are higher to employers than paid vacations. Our European counterparts have proven that a better-rested workforce results in higher productivity. And the health benefits and savings are not even worked into that equation—"

"That's my idea! He listened! He listened!"

"Shhh!"

"And so the committee will investigate implementing a law that mandates minimum paid vacation times for the U.S. worker. . . ."

We listen to the rest, stunned and silent. Because of Aidan, the president is asking a congressional committee to look into a mandatory vacation law. A chance meeting. An absurd thought from a kindergarten flunkie. And now this.

When the president signs off, Seth and Mira hoot and shout and hug Aidan. He hugs them back, smiling like he might never be able to stop. And then he looks at me.

"Congratulations, Aidan," I say.

His mouth is open, but no words come out.

"You don't have to say anything, Aidan. I know. Some things can't be explained."

We exit the store, leaving behind the smiling salesman, who doesn't seem to mind our brief, sale-less intrusion. He nods to me as I exit, and I offer an awkward nod in return, noting his thin dated tie that looks older than most of Langdon. Mira and Aidan walk ahead. She is still bubbling over with the news and rehashing every word. I can see the back of Aidan's head nodding, his arms flailing, filling in every gap.

"That sure is something, isn't it?" Seth says to me.

"I think the Universe of Truly Large Numbers just had to expand to accommodate that one."

"Nice that you didn't say anything."

"I didn't need to. Aidan said it for me. He had it written all over his face."

At the end of the street we spot a dog park. "Should we?" Seth asks.

"Why not?" I answer. "Lucky deserves a little play time." And I still need a little more time to face what is to come.

We let ourselves in through the gate, find an empty bench to sit on, and Seth unleashes Lucky. He is the hit of the dog park. He is instantly surrounded by three dogs wanting to herd him. He appears to enjoy the attention. He runs, carefree, his feet kicking, jumping, turning midair, driving the dogs trying to follow him into fits. He finally stops on a knoll in the middle of the park to munch on a thick tuft of grass, surrounded by befuddled, panting dogs. They don't know why they are compelled to chase Lucky. An ancient primal urge overpowers their domestic-flavor-of-the-month breeding.

"Lucky must be used to dogs."

"Maybe dogs herded the flock he came from."

"They didn't do a very good job, did they?"

"Or maybe Lucky just outsmarted them."

"Yeah, I bet that's it," Seth says proudly, like he raised Lucky himself.

Mira crosses her arms. "Instead of running Lucky ragged, he's running those pooches ragged. Looks like everyone's getting justice today."

Seth looks at his watch. "Not everyone. It's getting late. We better get going. Des still needs to set a few things straight."

I exhale. And the old Destiny is back.

29

AIDAN AND MIRA WAIT in the park with Lucky while Seth and I go to retrieve the car. I find myself counting the lines in the sidewalk as we walk. Counting my breaths. Counting the clicks of our steps. Searching for yet another thing to count, something I should count, and losing track of them all, wondering if I have finally, truly lost my mind. Or maybe the opposite—maybe today all the days, tears, waiting, and numbers are adding up to something just right. Something fair. It could be. If I am careful. If I don't stray too far this way or that. *Fourteen, fifteen, sixteen . . .*

"Nervous?"

I catch my breath. "No. Of course not. What's there to be nervous about?"

"Hey." Seth stops and squeezes my arm. "It's a good

decision, Des. You wanted a fair day. This will be part of it."

"I know, Seth. I know." Instead of the firmness I intended, I hear the rattling breathiness of my voice, like I am already vanishing because of my choice. His grip remains tight on my arm, and I'm glad he doesn't let go. It feels safe, like as long as he holds on, I can't disappear. Is that what I'm doing? I look up at him. "I'm okay. Just out of breath. Your legs are longer than mine. Let's slow down." He nods and we resume at a slower pace.

"Do you think they'll be angry when they see you?"

My parents. Angry? Hardly. "No," I answer. "I don't rate enough importance for anger."

"But you *are* angry."

"Maybe. I wonder what that says about me. I guess I don't have my priorities straight like they do."

"And cynical."

"Think so?" I smile, a tight deliberate smile, to top off my pessimism. "Aren't you angry at your parents for abandoning you?"

"They haven't exactly abandoned me, Des. It's only been two months, and it was my decision too. I mean, eventually everyone has to move away from their parents, right? It's normal. Part of growing up. A lot of kids count the days until they can get a little freedom."

"Well, I got to grow up at the ripe age of seven."

"Is that when they sent you off?"

I hear the disbelief in his voice. I look away and nod. He is probably already reevaluating me, wondering what makes me so repugnant.

"Some people really stink at being parents. You don't need a license, you know?"

"A license might not be a bad idea."

"But you at least have your aunt Edie. That's her name, right?"

Aunt Edie. Because no child should be alone. Everyone needs someone. "Yes. At least I have her." She's everything an aunt should be. Understanding, fun, a good listener. The ideal aunt.

"She's always been there for me," I tell him. "At least as much as she can be, considering that my parents bounce me around from boarding school to boarding school—always at a great distance from her. She tried to get custody of me once. She loves me that much. She's poor, but she has a little farm and an extra bedroom—a perfect place for a child to grow up—a pond and ducks and everything. But my parents wouldn't hear of it. Too humiliating, I suppose. But she would have me if she could."

"She sounds great. I'm sorry I missed her at the parents' day picnic. Did she come?"

"Yes. Of course she came. But she and I didn't sit with everyone else. We took a long walk. We don't get to see each other often, so we'd rather spend the time alone."

"Why was she coming today?"

All this talking, it's going in directions I can't control. Another reason why it is best to stay to yourself. Why leaving Hedgebrook was too risky. At least the routine there was safe.

"A visit. Only a visit."

"I guess in some ways it turned out okay, after all. If she had come today, you wouldn't have come to rescue me, and we wouldn't be here right now. You'd probably be off with her somewhere instead."

"Rescuing? I'd hardly call it that."

"Was to me. How long have you had the car? Was it a gift?"

Now would be the time to tell. Before I dig myself in any deeper. But it is his own doing, really. He assumes too much. I never said it was mine exactly. One should never assume. It only gets you into trouble. The end of the day is just as good a time to tell as now. *But he's asking now.* Outright asking. "Seth—"

"Yes?"

"Today. I just got it today. It was a surprise."

"A guilt gift from your parents?"

"Yes. That must be it."

We are almost back to the car. Last sidewalk lines. Last steps. Last breaths. So important. And I'm missing it all. *Seventeen, eighteen . . .*

"What are you counting?"

I walk faster. How could he know? "I wasn't counting anything."

"I saw your lips moving."

"It was a song. I was humming a song."

"No, you weren't. It was numbers."

"Drop it, Seth."

He breathes out a loud grumbling breath. "Like everything else? Why do you always have to push everyone away?"

I walk five steps, three breaths, two sidewalk lines before I answer. "If you knew me. If you got close. You might vanish."

"*Vanish?* That's crazy."

I stop. He gives me the look again. The demented look. The fragile-twit look. I prefer scorn. I can gain strength from that. Fragility weakens me.

"Des, I didn't mean—"

I begin to walk on, but he grabs me and pulls me into the

shadow of a storefront nook. His hands firmly grip both of my arms. "Destiny, I don't care what you were doing. You could be reciting the periodic table in pig latin for all I care. I was just trying to connect with you. Is that so bad?"

He is a head taller than me and so close I must tilt my head back to see him fully. I feel the heat of his fingers on my arms. The tautness of my neck muscles. What was his question? So bad? My knees are shaky. Hot. And yet they continue to bear my weight. His face is close. Ten inches. His lips part. His head tilts. Nine inches. Eight. Seven. My chest is on fire. Six. Five. I turn away, my eyes looking down at the ground beside me. Four. The unholy number. He retreats. His hands drop from my arms.

"Mira and Aidan are waiting," I say.

He steps back, looks away like he sees something at the end of the street, his eyes narrowing, his hands shoving into his pockets, and then he looks back. "And Lucky too," he adds. He looks away again briefly and then turns back with a smile. Close to a smirk but a smile, nonetheless.

An offering. At least a truce.

And at that moment, for that unearned smile, I would gladly tell him every thought and secret that was ever in my head. But of course, he wouldn't really want to know them. We all think we know what we want until it is too late.

30

EAST. I KNOW TO GO EAST.

"That way," I tell Seth. The buildings of Langdon become scattered and few. Houses. None of them familiar. The wind is brisk. We should put the top up. Can a season turn in just one day? In just a few hours? We pass fields of golden flowers. Forests of birch. White rail fences. The colors, angles, and memories of home. But it isn't. Not anymore. After today, it will never be mine again.

"Another toast!" Mira says. We stopped for cherry slushes at the market, and now Mira has turned the simple act of drinking into yet another game—anything to keep out the silence and keep us bonded. We have already toasted Mrs. Wicket, Lucky, the president, and

☼

the Victorymobile, as she has now dubbed the car. What could be left to toast?

"Here's to Miss Boggs and miscounting tests!"

"Here's to Bingham and comb-overs!"

"Here's to bloody noses!"

Seth and Aidan seem as enthusiastic as Mira. I raise my cherry slush. "If we're really going to toast our reasons for being here, we must include Mr. Nestor."

They all lift their cups. "To Mr. Nestor and fair days!"

I finish my drink. So does Seth, and he passes his empty cup to me. I stack them together and shove them beneath my seat. This will surely put an end to Mira's toasting.

"Who do you think Mr. Nestor really is?" she asks.

"A serial killer," I answer. "That's what I told him."

Seth laughs. "Sure. He systematically kills his students by boring them to death? We already have one of those at Hedgebrook. Bingham. We don't need another one."

"He was probably just a sub," Aidan says.

"Lost in the garden?"

"No. Ditching like you."

"Right," I answer. Aidan can never quite let go of his concrete world. But, then again, I can never quite let go of the one I am in either. It's disconcerting to think that he and I might be a good balance.

"Which way now?" Seth asks.

I look at the crossroad. "Straight," I answer. "No, left. Left."

"Are you sure?"

"Yes." I think.

The road becomes narrower and curves and bends. Houses are set back, mostly obscured by acres of foliage.

"Pricey part of town," Aidan observes.

"This the way?" Seth asks.

I nod. But I am not sure. How can I tell him I don't exactly remember where my house is? I was eight the last time I was here, and eight-year-olds don't pay attention to directions. It is not streets and road names that matter to children, but landmarks, like a windmill, a rusted-out wagon, a long row of mailboxes, twin stone pillars with lion sculptures topping them. Where are these guideposts?

The road twists and dips, winds and curves.

And stops. We are at a dead end. No house.

The car idles. "I don't think this is it," Seth says. "Unless your parents live in a rabbit hole."

"Why don't you ask directions?" Mira asks.

We all turn and look at her. We are in the middle of nowhere, and there is no one around. Mira shrugs. Point taken.

"I'm sorry," I say. "We must have made a wrong turn."

"No problem," Seth says, turning around the car. "What did you say the address was again?"

"It's 829 Ravenwood."

We backtrack to the last cross street we passed, and Seth stops and looks both ways. He looks at me. I shake my head. I want to slide beneath the seat with the empty cups. What seventeen-year-old doesn't know where her house is?

Seth eases out onto the road. "Let's try—"

"Over there!" Aidan's arm juts between us and points to the right. "There's someone."

Several yards down the road, an elderly man with a wide-brimmed hat sits in a chair between two baskets. One holds apples, and the other, bunches of miniature sunflowers. A sign facing our direction reads: FRIUT AND FLOWRS 4 SAEL.

"Funny. I didn't notice him when we passed by before."

"Poor old guy," Mira says. "Not too much business way out here in the boonies."

"Wait here." I hop out and run over to him to ask directions. "Excuse me? Do you know—"

He waves his hands and shakes his head. "No English. No English. Flowers? Flowers?"

I try my rusty French. He repeats: "No English. No English. Apples?"

My almost nonexistent German.

"No English. No English. Cheap. Cheap."

I walk back to the car.

"That was fast. What did he say?" Seth asks.

"He doesn't speak English or any language that I recognize. Maybe we'll find someone else—"

Seth puts the car in park and opens his door. "Let me give it a shot."

We watch Seth talking with the old man. I see the same gestures he gave me. No. No. No. And then suddenly the old man smiles. He laughs and stands and gives Seth a hearty slap on the shoulder. Many nods. Laughter. It is like they are old friends. He pulls an apple from the basket, rubs it on his shirt, and gives it to Seth. They shake hands, and Seth returns to the car.

"What was that all about?" I ask.

"Tagalog. The old guy speaks Tagalog."

"What!" Aidan says.

"Did he give you directions?"

"Yep. Second left. Veer right at the fork. First left."

☼

"Tagalog," Aidan mumbles. "We're lost, and the only person in sight speaks Tagalog, which Seth happens to know."

Mira, Seth, and I look at each other. Mira's brows rise. Aidan is speaking to his lap, not us. The universe and its numbers are clearly expanding at much too fast a rate for him.

Seth puts the car into gear. "Hold on," I say. I open the glove box, grab three of the hundred-dollar bills, and jump out of the car. A few yards away, I turn and call back to the others. "We're his only customers. It should be his fair day too, right?"

The old man's jaw drops as I place the three bills in his hand. I choose a small bunch of sunflowers from his basket and run away before he can stop me. As soon as I jump back in the car, Seth heads down the road.

Mira offers one more toast. "Here's to sunflowers and directions!"

Seth turns at the second left. The road is narrow, trees hugging close, their fallen leaves providing a carpet of orange and yellow for us to drive on. Still not recognizable. "Very generous of you," Seth finally says. "Why do you carry so much money in your glove box? It's not the safest place, you know?"

"Especially with a convertible," Mira adds.

Aidan grunts. "But I bet the old guy is glad that you keep it there. He can quit for the day."

I shift in my seat. I glance sideways at Seth. "The money?" My fingers run through Lucky's woolen coat. "Oh, the money. That. It's there because. Well. It's not exactly mine."

"What do you mean, it's not *yours*?" Seth asks. "You're carrying somebody else's money around in your car? And spending it?" I notice his last three words are an octave higher.

The world dims. Can time stand still? In these few seconds, I am convinced it can—that the world really can defy logic. At least the logic we know. That the unexplainable is part of the science that makes the world spin, like mystery is the blood running through its veins. I move forward and backward in time at lightning speed, thinking, weighing, remembering, while the three of them are caught in a timeless fog. We've come so far since this morning. *Nice car, Des. Can Aidan come? Whose car? Go. Go.*

And then time circles back around, the way it always does. It catches the gear that left it suspended, and there is no way around it. "I have a secret."

Mira is delighted. "More points for Des! I love secrets!" Her smile disappears as she leans close and whispers, "Is this a real one, Des?"

"Wise up, Mira," Aidan says. "Most likely she's going to tell us she has *two* baboon hearts—a spare that she carries in her purse."

"This one's true, Mira," I say. "Not that the others, weren't."

Mira nods. "Of course."

"Okay." I take a deep breath. "I'll just lay it out: I don't know who this car belongs to. It's not mine. I simply found it with the engine running and—"

"What?"

Seth slams on the brakes and swerves to the shoulder of the road. He and Aidan are both spouting a string of curses. Seth gets out of the car and slams the door. He walks to the front of the car, slapping his forehead, and then slams his hands down on the hood. *"Are you nuts?"*

"Seth!" Mira yells.

"Do you know what she's done?" Aidan yells back.

"She's stolen a car!"

"We've stolen a car!"

"We need to listen—"

"Don't act so high and mighty! You know you suspected something before now!"

"Suspected something! Yeah! Like borrowing a car, not *stealing* it!"

"Our faces are probably already plastered in post offices!"

"Can we say we borrowed it?"

"We're accessories!"

They're all shouting over each other and not leaving me any space to explain.

"Please!"

Baaaa!

Lucky jumps up on the dash, disturbed at the commotion, and for a brief moment, they are silenced.

"Listen to me!" I yell. "Let me explain! Can't you see? We were meant to have this car! It was there waiting for us! The door was even open! I swear!" I throw open my door and step out and find myself passionately pleading for the day. I have never passionately pleaded for anything in my life, and the more I plead, the more I am energized. It feels suspiciously and deliriously wonderful. Delirious? *Is that what they think I am?* Maybe so. It runs through me like a spiked fever. I talk in a loud frenzied stream so they can't stop me. "Look at today! The four of us! Aidan and the president! Lucky in the road! The car! The money in the glove box! It's a fair day! *Our* fair day! Something happened. Maybe it was Mr. Nestor. Or something in the air. Or my calendar. Or something else. I don't know. But this day was made for us!"

Seth walks around to my side of the car, his face almost comical in its sputtering anger. He leans close. "Listen to me! Listen very carefully. There is no such thing as a fair day, Destiny! Check in to planet Earth for once in your life! We took a car! Somebody *else's* car! A damn nice car!" His eyelids flutter, and he takes a deep slow breath. It makes three veins in his neck pop out. "What we did is called *grand theft auto*." He points and glares at the front seat. "And now look! It even has a hole in the seat!" His hands squeeze against the sides of his head as he walks in circles. "Destruction of property! Grand theft!" His hands shoot upward. "Expulsion won't begin to cover this! A hole in the leather seat! A gaping hole!" I notice he is beginning to sound a little delirious himself. He stops and glares at me. "How is *that* fair?" He shakes his head. "You are so disconnected from the real world it's pathetic! You pretend like you're there, but you're really invisible. The real Des never shows her face except when she gets caught and—"

"Stop right there! Don't you dare lecture me about connection, Seth Marshall Kaplan!" I derive great pleasure in his dropped jaw. "That's right! I know your middle name and a hell of a lot more! I have *your number*, Seth. Some people are easy to figure. Aidan and Mira, they wear their neuroses all over their faces. But you took me longer to figure out, and I finally realized *why*." Now he looks worried. Good. I move closer. "You're not that different from me. You just wear a different kind of invisibility. You fly under the radar, all right. That smoothness, your easy smile. But you're a chameleon. You're whatever you need to be at the moment so you can fit in. At least I'm consistent!"

"It's true, Seth," Mira says. "You do have an easy smile."

Aidan's face screws up. "Neuroses?"

Seth sputters for a moment. Is it embarrassment or anger I see in his eyes? He turns away and walks back to the other side of the car. "We're going back!" He pulls open his door.

"Stop! Wait!" Desperation pricks at my back. "Here! I have another coincidence for you!"

Aidan cuts me off. "No more coincidences!"

Seth chimes in, his voice thick with sarcasm. "Just what we need! *Another* story!"

"*Please. Just listen.*"

"Not a chance!"

"We're out of here!"

"Stop! Both of you!" Mira says. She leans over the seat and snatches the keys from the ignition. Her voice is a growl. "*I* want to hear. So we *are* going to listen! Go, Des."

Mira's fierce posture catches them off guard. I make my case fast.

"On December 5, 1664, a ship sank off the coast of Wales. There were eighty-one passengers on board, but only one survived. His name was Hugh Williams. Over a hundred years later, on December 5, 1785, another ship sank in the same place. All sixty aboard drowned, except for one passenger. His name was Hugh Williams. And then on December 5, 1860, in the very same waters, another ship sank. There were no survivors except for one person."

I don't have to finish the last sentence of my story. I can see it on Aidan's and Seth's faces.

"Hugh Williams," Seth finally says.

I nod. "That's right. And you can't blame it on the Law of Truly Large Numbers. The universe isn't that old or that big! Sometimes there's a destiny that we can't understand. Unimaginable things happen. Far stranger things than a car being at our disposal. Nothing has changed from this morning, when you wanted to come with me, except that now I've been honest with you."

Seth rolls his eyes and looks at Aidan. They both look at Mira, who is still clutching the keys in her fist. She appears to be deep in concentration. She pinches her chin.

"It might be wise for us to name our children Hugh Williams, don't you think?" She looks sideways at Aidan and winks. "All three of them."

Aidan tries to maintain his scowl, but the magic of Mira weakens him. He grins and shrugs. "I suppose we're already in trouble. No one's come looking for the car yet. What can a few more hours hurt?"

Seth sighs, turns, and throws his hands up in the air, a captain facing mutiny. He whips around sharply to face me again, still breathing hard, like he has just run a marathon. He is not happy that I have exposed him. His eyes narrow. He smiles. Not a happy smile but like a cat who has cornered a mouse. "I'm the only one who can drive. So before we go anywhere, I declare a game."

"A game?" I don't have a good feeling about this.

"Truth or dare."

Not good at all. "What's the dare?"

"We drive straight to the market in Langdon and you call Hedgebrook. You tell them you took the car."

"And kidnapped us," Aidan slips in.

Not so bad. He's an amateur at this, really. I lean forward, bracing myself against the car. "And the truth?"

"An easy one, that is, if you have the same guts to tell the truth as you do to steal a car."

"I do." I think.

"What's the big deal about this day? October 19. What's the secret?"

An easy one?

Hardly.

Unexplainable. Illogical. Impossible. Yes. But at the same time, real. Very real for me. A day I was rejected. Sent away. Separated. A day I should have said good-bye. A day I should have taken different steps. A day I turned seven. Not easy at all, Seth. But I must get home today. Tell them. Tell my parents. Has the courage suddenly materialized? Or the foolishness? I am not sure. But I must get home. A measure of truth could get me there.

"Truth, Des." It is like Seth can see the workings of my mind, as I search for something plausible to substitute for the truth, and he is trying to trip me up. *Truth, Des. Truth.* A measure.

"Today is my birthday."

They are silent, their faces blank, like they were expecting something else.

"That would make the day special," Mira says.

"Yes, that's right."

"Of course."

There they go again. Assuming. Not a wise thing to do.

There are many meanings to *special,* and they aren't all good. Different. Odd. Rare. Uncommon. Peculiar. Yes, special. Like special circumstances in a crime that can up a life sentence to a death sentence. Yes, that kind of special.

"The nineteenth."

"Oh."

It is obvious that their minds and mouths are out of sync. Minds racing. Mouths tripping.

"You and your mom share the same birthday?" Seth's voice has suddenly gone soft.

"That's right."

"Today is your birthday," Aidan repeats like he is trying to process what that means.

Mira leans over the door and hugs me. Her eyes glisten. "Happy birthday, Des."

31

SETH DRIVES AT A SLOW and easy pace. No one tries to fill the silence. For the moment the wrinkles between us are patted out. The universe is large. The breakable is real. Momentum is our fuel. I watch for landmarks.

He veers to the right at the fork. Just ahead, a weathered windmill stands at the far end of a field, its blades turning in the breeze. My stomach twists. A short distance farther, a neat row of mailboxes hugs the road. White, red, black, and silver. This is it.

We are coming up fast on another lane. I see it already. A street sign, shorter than I remember: RAVENWOOD. Raised metal letters that I always wanted to jump up and touch, like touching them would help me understand my place in the world, but I was too small to reach. Seth sees the sign and steers the car to the left, down a narrow lane that is crowded with golden birches on either side.

We could turn back now and life would go on as before. As it always has. Return, go back, and not move on—as I have always not moved on except to a new boarding school where no one knew me or wanted to know me. Turn back and Mr. Gardian would take care of the misdeeds of the day as he always has. And as always, Mother and Father would not be disturbed. Turn back. Because no good can come from this day. It's not too late, Des. Turn back. But we are being swallowed up by a tunnel of golden birches and momentum that won't let us go.

"I don't see any addresses."

"I don't see any houses."

And then, set back a hundred feet on a brick drive littered with leaves are two stone pillars, the lions still crouched and poised—landmarks that have been waiting for me. Just below them is a small, distinguished realty sign.

"Here," I say. "Turn here."

The large wrought-iron gate that spans the drive has been pulled back to allow access.

"Was that a for-sale sign we just passed?" Aidan asks.

"Looked like it to me," Seth confirms.

"Your parents are moving without telling you?" Mira asks.

"I knew."

The birches grow thinner, the lane widens. Trimmed hedges appear. Tidy flower beds. And we are still on the driveway.

"Is this the drive just to your house?" Aidan asks.

"Yes."

The birches are finally pushed back and lawns appear. Still farther ahead, the house finally looms.

"Holy—" but Seth doesn't finish his sentence.

"I knew you came from money—heck, we all do—but this . . ." Aidan doesn't finish his sentence either.

The grandeur that cut me off seems to have cut everyone else short too.

"That is some house!"

Except Mira.

"Yes, Mira, it is. Or was."

Baaa. Baaa.

Seth reaches over and rubs Lucky's head. "Yeah, fella, there's plenty of snacking to be had on those lawns."

Mira lays her hand on my shoulder. She knows I don't like such displays. "Des, you okay?"

"Of course I am." Now kindly remove your hand. No. Keep it there. Please keep it there.

"You're hardly breathing," she says. "And, look—your knuckles are white."

I look down at my hands, balled into tight fists, and I force them to relax. I breathe as Mira instructed me. My house. I am at *my* house. For the first time in nine years.

32

WE FOLLOW THE ROAD around to the house. Past fountains that no longer run. Past an apple orchard. Past flower gardens long past their bloom. Past arbors, pathways, and gazebos that were once my playground. The wind whips my face, my skirt, throwing dust in my eyes, like it is telling me to go away.

Close your eyes.

Don't look, Destiny.

Don't look.

But I did.

I do.

I dab at my eyes, trying to rub away the grit that makes them tear. But I don't stop looking. Because I never have. Looking forward. Looking back. Wondering how many steps, minutes, days, and breaths add up to just the right number. There has to be a way to make things right. There has to be. I won't run away. Today they will listen to me, and I will say all the things I should have said long ago.

Seth stops off to the side of the house just before we reach the front portico and the intricately inlaid drive of slate and brick. "Still want to do this?"

Mira leans forward, her face contorted like she just received bad news. "Des, dear, I'm afraid no one is home. It looks deserted."

"Let's go in."

Seth puts the car in park and turns off the engine. "What about Lucky?"

I nod toward the southern lawn. "Let him graze. The hedges will keep him in."

"Come on, boy." Seth picks up Lucky and carries him to the lawn that is overgrown just enough to be a little lamb's paradise.

Aidan slams the car door behind us, and the sound echoes off the deserted landscape.

"Quiet out here, isn't it?" Mira is obviously spooked by the loneliness.

We walk up the rest of the driveway, up the three curved steps, and I try the door. It's unlocked. I push it open.

Seth catches up and, along with us, peers inside. For a moment, time is suspended, held back by the threshold of the massive door. I hear the heart of the house. *Thump, thump, thump.* It beats in my chest.

"Wow," Mira says, breaking the spell.

"Should we knock?" Aidan asks.

I look at him sharply. "It *is* my house, Aidan."

I step inside and they follow. I look up at the ceiling, the double curving staircase, and at the vase of fresh white gladiolas on the pedestal to the left. I smile. The flowers had to be the Realtor's touch—a stab of warmth in a cold empty house. Or could it be Mother's idea? In honor of my birthday? Is it possible? *Today could be different. It could add up to everything right.* I snap off one flower and tuck it behind my ear.

The living room is unchanged, except for one piece of missing furniture, the white grand piano along with its bench. Mr. Gardian saved that for me.

"Anybody home?" Mira calls sheepishly. "Mrs. Faraday?"

"Shhh," I tell her. "Let's go upstairs. I'll show you my room."

We move toward the stairs, Mira's peep-toed platforms *click, click, click*ing on the marble tiles.

"Why am I not surprised to see you here, Destiny?"

Mira jumps. I turn around.

I recognize the voice before I even see him. "You know me too well, Mr. Gardian," I answer.

He takes a few steps closer, joining us in the foyer. "I suppose after all these years I do. And this time I see you brought some partners in crime." He sighs quite deliberately to make his point. "So, how much is this one going to cost me?"

"You mean me, don't you?"

"Yes. You."

"Probably a bundle. My parents about?"

"Destiny. Please. You know it's not good to—"

"Never mind. Not surprised they're gone. It's only my birthday. Typical."

Seth steps forward. "Sir, very sorry about the intrusion. The day just got started off on the wrong foot. Destiny's aunt Edie had some problems with her tires—"

"Aunt Edie?" Mr. Gardian looks from Seth to me. "*Destiny*. She's not back in the picture, is she?"

"Relax, Mr. Gardian. She didn't show. I just came to give my friends the nickel tour. Can you please just give us a few minutes?" He folds his arms slowly across his chest and throws in a frown for good measure. "For old time's sake?" I add.

His arms drop to his sides, and he finally nods. He moves awkwardly toward me and kisses the top of my head. "Happy birthday, Destiny," he whispers. I close my eyes briefly, which allows the ache in my throat to spread to my chest. He steps back and shakes his head. "I had a little something delivered for you to Hedgebrook today. I'm sorry you weren't there to receive it."

"You know I don't celebrate my birthday."

"But I think it's about time you did."

"We'll be going back soon. I'm sure Mrs. Wicket has set it aside for me."

He smiles. "Just a few minutes now. Escrow closes today. The Realtor will be here shortly to sign the last papers." He lowers his voice to a whisper. "And I don't want any scenes or anything, all right?"

I whisper back to him. "My friends can still hear you, Mr. Gardian."

"Right."

"Nice to meet you, Mr. Gardian." Seth reaches his hand out to shake like they are old buddies. Smooth.

"Edward. Edward Farrell," Mr. Gardian says. "Mr. Gardian is just Destiny's pet name for me. I've gotten used to it."

"Oh. I see." But it is clear he doesn't see. Smooth Seth is

caught off guard. I love being me sometimes. Not often. But sometimes.

Aidan and Mira say their hellos and good-byes too, and they follow me toward the stairs.

"Why do you call him Mr. Gardian when his name is Farrell?" Seth asks.

"He's lying. His name *is* Gardian. Even my parents call him that. You can't believe everything people tell you."

"He seemed like a nice man," Mira says. "I'm surprised he would lie."

"He is a nice man," I tell her. "But nice people lie too. You should know that by now. Come on. Let's hurry before we all get thrown out. It's a habit around here."

I start up the stairs, noting the grain of the marble that's been etched in my memory for so long, remembering the pictures I thought I saw in the patterns when I was a child. A horse. A witch. An airplane. I don't see those pictures anymore, only a blurry swirl of gray and white. The others trail behind, but nevertheless I can hear the gasps from Mira and the whispered comments from Aidan. A few from Seth too.

"This place is huge."

"Did you see the living room?"

"More like a ballroom."

"It was a ballroom."

"All of Hedgebrook could fit in this place."

"Why would they move?"

"It looks like they moved a long time ago."

"I don't think so."

"Or their housekeeper is lousy."

"Did you see that cobweb on the chandelier?"

"Shhh. Her parents might be here and hear you."

"I don't think anyone's home. Except that Farrell fellow."

Mira catches up with me. "Where are we going, Des?"

"I told you. My bedroom."

We walk down a hallway. Past Mother and Father's room. Past the nursery. Past the playroom, and we arrive at my door. That is, if it is still my door. If the contents haven't been thrown out the way the occupant was.

I fear I might crumble or do something else just as embarrassing as I turn the knob and push open the door, but instead just the opposite happens. I am infused with the energy and life the room once held, lifted like a child onto someone's shoulders. The room is just as it was. Just as I remember it, but better. Not a piece of furniture has been moved. It is a shrine to a child who was supposed to make the world whole.

I cross to the bed, an elaborate canopied affair with wispy sheers as sweet and pink as cotton candy, tied back with pink bows at the posts. I slide my hand over the vermicelli quilted spread, pink roses bordering the edges, not as soft as it once was, stiffer with age, but still beautiful. I sit on the bed and bounce. I laugh. The dust swirls in my eyes again, making them burn and water, and I use the heel of my hand to wipe the tears away.

"This room is very . . . pink," Seth comments.

"What's with all the ruffles and bows?" Aidan adds.

"It's . . . sweet," Mira says, but the way she says *sweet* is distasteful, like saccharine sweet. Not-quite-right sweet. Aftertaste sweet. This from a girl with flashy peep-toed platforms and a poodle skirt.

There is nothing wrong with this room. Nothing. But the moment has passed. Now I see it through their eyes. I run across the room to the shelf that once held my Madame Alexander dolls. Gone. I glide my palm over the dusty shelf. Maybe in a moment of guilt, someone thought to pack them away. Or maybe they were discarded when I was. My fingers curl, gathering the shelf dust into my fist. "Seth, do you really believe there's no such thing as a fair day?"

Seth steps closer to me. "Destiny—"

"Just one day—"

"It's not—"

"Forget it! It doesn't matter!" I grab two books from the shelf below and throw them across the room. I grab two more and still more, flinging them everywhere. My bed, the walls, the furniture, glass lamps on tabletops sent sprawling and crashing to the floor.

"Destiny! Stop!" Seth springs on me from behind and holds me so both of my arms are pinned beneath his.

"Let go!" I yell, but he holds tight.

Aidan is pale, looking nervously at the door and the shattered glass. "I think this might be what Mr. Farrell meant by no scenes."

"Gardian!" I scream. "His name is Gardian!"

"Pipe it, Aidan!" Mira says.

A scene. Yes, that's what I'm making. And that has never gotten me what I wanted. It only made things worse, then and now. I relax against Seth's chest, feeling tired and limp, like he is all that is holding me up. He leans close, his breath warm against my neck and ear. "Is it safe to let go?" he whispers. I nod.

His arms loosen and slowly fall away, like he doesn't quite trust me. Mira steps closer and takes one of my hands in hers. "Des, I'm so sorry. Everyone's had their fair day but you. You wanted to come see your parents, get some things off your chest, and now you can't. It's wrong. It's just plain wrong. If there were some way—"

"I know where they moved to. It's not far from here."

Mira brightens. "Then let's go."

"The sooner the better," Aidan says. "Before Mr. Far"—he shoots a furtive glance my way—"I mean, before Mr. Gardian sees this mess."

Seth nods toward the door. "Let's go." But as Aidan and Mira tiptoe out, he hangs back, holding my arm.

"Des, about what I said. Back there. You know, about checking in to planet Earth, and the nuts stuff. I don't think you're nuts. Really. I was just scared. And maybe a little angry. But, yes, I think there are days that are something like fair. Where things add up the way they should. Where the good guys win. One whole day could be that way. Why not? Maybe it's just us making it that way. You know, trying harder or something. Or maybe it's something else that we don't understand, like the Hugh Williams thing. Weird stuff that we can't explain. Maybe everything doesn't have to be explained. But from the minute I got in the car with you this morning, I knew the day was different. That it was going to be one of those once-in-a-lifetime days." He pulls me closer. "And I'm not trying to be smooth and say the things you want to hear. I'm being honest with you. Today is one of those kind of days. Your parents need to hear what you have to say. Maybe it could change things—"

"I can't do this, Seth. I can't. I can't do it. You don't understand. I was wrong about everything. We need to go back. Just like you said. We need to go back. We need—"

"Des, we've come this far. Don't back down now." He grabs both of my arms and holds me steady. "We'll be with you."

33

WE'VE COME THIS FAR.

So far. But the place we've traveled to is not a safe place. It's not just a place on a map but a place buried deep in my past. An angry place, and a shameful one. A place that no one could lead me to before this day. Why do I push everyone away? Seth asks that like he is the first one. How can anyone expect a child to know that answer? It's like asking why you eat or breathe. You do it because you always have. You do it to survive. How could a seven-year-old know? But it didn't keep them from asking.

This far.

A road trip got me here. A road trip that wasn't meant to happen. But somehow it did. Because I made it happen, as Seth says? Or because of a visiting teacher in a garden?

Or a calendar page dropped into a waste can? But the road trip isn't over. I still have farther to travel. *You can do it, Des.* Can I? Will my parents finally hear me? Could they possibly listen? Is it that kind of day? A once-in-a-lifetime sort of day? Can I make time rewind and play itself out differently? Four of us. Me. Seth. Mira. Aidan. Four. The unholy number. Or the whole number. Which is it?

Seth quietly gathers up Lucky, and we head out. Down the drive. Down the road. Past thick stands of birch, their leaves shivering in the breeze. Past the gate and stone lions. Two? Three? Four? Which is it? We are moving too fast to count. I stop trying. Silence and the air of a late October day gallop past us. The car stops and idles at Ravenwood. I point to the right before Seth can ask.

Ravenwood curves and quickly opens up to a patchwork of hills, vistas, and emptiness.

"Pretty hills," Mira says, breaking the silence. The hills are brown.

"I don't see any houses," Aidan observes.

No houses. Only empty brown hills that all belong to me. We reach the end of Ravenwood, and I point to the left. Seth turns without comment.

Only a short distance down the road, we come to the beginning of a low stone wall and then an ornate gate, green with weather and age. These landmarks I remember.

"Here," I say.

The road climbs up a hill. The highest hill in Langdon. The engine revs.

You can do this, Destiny.

But I never could before. Why now? I ruffle the petals of the flowers in my lap, and brush the peacock feather against my cheek. So soft. Baby soft. Like a whisper. *Give Mama a nice good-bye. Give your brother a kiss.* The road narrows and zigzags back and forth, edged by plateaus that are dotted with stony memorials, clustered together like families.

"Where the—"

"Quiet, Aidan. Please," I whisper. I hear music. Music I have shut out all these years but that still clings to the hills and always will. Mother's favorite song. The lullaby she loves and struggled to learn on the piano, but now it is played by bagpipes. Long wispy notes. Lingering. Rolling over the hills like fog, hiding between the stones, circling around and around all these years waiting for me.

Seth clears his throat. "Is this—"

"All the way to the top," I say.

We arrive at the crest. A hundred yards off, another landmark, a crooked oak.

"Here," I tell him. "Park here. We have to walk the rest of the way."

Seth stops the car and turns off the engine. No one moves.

"Come on, boys," Mira finally says. "You heard her. Let's walk."

I step out and head toward the crooked oak, one of its branches split away by a long-ago lightning storm. A low iron fence comes into view, its curly grillwork an odd contrast to the barren landscape. The gate swings back and forth in the wind, the squeaking hinges swirling with the music already in my head. The others follow close behind.

I stop at the gate. Seth stops on one side of me, Mira and Aidan on the other. Within the small fenced area, the grass still holds a hint of green, like the warmth of the occupants keeps winter at bay. I look at the chiseled stones, the granite as new and cold now as it was ten years ago. Ten years ago today. Father's stone first, then Mother's, and finally Gavin's. Baby Gavin's. Forever their baby.

"This is where my family is now."

No one speaks. I am not sure they even breathe. Just like those on the other side of the gate.

"I'm sorry I didn't tell you."

Still no answer.

"I couldn't," I add.

Seth takes a step forward, squeezing past me, through the gate, stepping into the world of Mother, Father, and Gavin. Mira and Aidan follow him. I stand behind the gate, a boundary I have never crossed, looking through the spaces of their backs, arms, and elbows, looking at my past etched in stone and letters and dates. Permanent dates that don't change. Real. It hasn't changed. I couldn't change anything. This day couldn't change anything either.

"You weren't abandoned," Seth whispers. "You were left behind."

Exactly. And all the denying, counting, and retracing of steps can't undo it. It can only add up to what it is—as Seth said, left behind. Pain twists in my chest like a knife. I whisper Seth's words. "Left behind." The knife twists deeper. It feels good. Necessary. Deserved.

"Oh, my God," Mira whispers. "Today is the day they died. All of them."

"October 19." Aidan's voice is uneven.

"On your birthday," Seth says. I see the back of his head gently shaking.

Mira gasps. "And your mother's too. She died on her birthday."

"You were only seven?"

The wind plucks at the branches of the oak. The gate squeaks. The bagpipes play. Music that played so long ago and has waited for me in these hollows, hills, and stones. Music that, for a seven-year-old, was frightening and loud, and yet now as I listen, it is as soft and hesitant as a tear trickling down a cheek. I turn my head to the side, trying to catch every note. I wonder what trick of time and perspective has made the music change.

Seth reaches forward as if to touch Father's stone, but then pulls back. He shakes his head more vigorously. "What are the chances?"

"A million to one, at least," I answer. "But it's bound to happen to someone. That's the Law of Truly Large Numbers, right?"

Aidan turns to face me. "Destiny. . . ." I have never quite seen anyone's face look the way his does right now, chiseled and frozen, like it might break if he moves one more centimeter. Mira and Seth turn to face me too, all of them on one side of a boundary and me on the other, just like that day.

"I watched them get on the plane. They were late because of me, you know? I refused to say good-bye. I made a terrible fuss—"

"Des, you were only seven—"

"They finally had to leave without a good-bye from me. That's all Mother wanted. After they left, I ran to the window. I was going to wave. I really was. I was looking for Mother and Father in the passenger windows. But just as the plane started pulling out, an incoming plane lost an engine and veered into them. I saw it all. The flash. The explosion. Everything. All the chances stacked up in the worst possible way."

Seth steps closer to me. "You could have told us, Destiny."

I laugh. "How? This is the first time I've admitted it to myself. I always thought—" I close my eyes. Hope. It was desperate hope. Obsessive hope. Irrational hope. But hope. The only hope I had. A chance to be redeemed from the unthinkable and the unforgivable. And if chances could stack up one way, given enough time, maybe they could stack up the other way too.

But not this time. I open my eyes.

Mira sobs. Aidan holds her.

I feel calm. Disconnected. Like I am a thousand miles away, writing it all out on pink stationery, a distant numbness that keeps me safe and has always kept me safe. *Tuck it away, Destiny. Put it in your bottom drawer. No one will ever know.* But now they do. I look at Mira, her tears flowing, and my numb shell prickles away. I inhale a quick sharp breath, like it is my first. My fingers tremble.

Seth steps forward and takes my hand. "Maybe now's the time?"

I look in his eyes, uncertain, thousands of miles disappearing, my feet feeling the anchor of this spot. "Time for what?"

"You never said good-bye, Des. Maybe you need to." He tugs on my hand gently, pulling me forward toward the gate, and I finally understand his intention.

"No!"

He stops moving but doesn't let go. Mira steps forward and takes my other hand, her cheeks still wet with tears. "Destiny. You can tell them. Now." She whispers, like she is afraid she might disturb Mother and Father and the sleeping baby Gavin. "Tell them. Whatever you want. We'll stay with you."

I look past her at the stones. My eyes ache. I need to blink, but I can't. My lids are frozen open. *Tell them? Now? What?*

My feet move forward against my will. Or maybe because of it. I don't know. But I move, like I am floating. *One step. Two. Three.* At the entrance of the gate. *Four.*

Through it. *Five*. Mira holding one hand. Seth the other. *Six. Seven*. The holy number. They let go.

And I face my family.

Mother. Father. And sweet baby Gavin.

Nothing between me and them.

No glass. No airport gates. No time.

Just me. And them.

I step closer on my own. *My family*. My hand shakes as I reach out, and I steady it on Father's stone. Steady. Yes. Father was steady. He could lift me high above his head, and I was never afraid. My finger traces the groove of his name. William. Will. I feel his last kiss on my forehead. Warm. His smile trying to prod me from my sulking. I wanted to smile for him. I almost did. My hand skims the top of his marker, and it leads me to the next. Mother's stone. Caroline. Sable black hair that smelled of roses, silky strands tickling my nose as she held me. Always holding me. I touch the date on her stone. October 19. She had only thirty-five years before the day that brought her took her away again.

And Gavin. The shortest time of all. A chubby angel is carved into the top of his stone. I drop to my knees. Gavin. Could he possibly remember me pushing his pram? Singing for him when he cried? I did those things. I reach out and touch the sculpted angel that hovers above him. A baby should never be alone. Was this Mr. Gardian's touch? He always thought of everything. All these years I didn't know or thank him. A chubby angel for Gavin. All the things I should have said to Mr. Gardian, to Gavin, to my parents, to everyone, but never did.

Tell them.

I hear Mira's sniffles. I never cried for them. Like telling and admitting, crying would make it real. It would show acceptance, and some things should not be accepted, but the logic that has sustained me vanished when I stepped through this gate. Here I am. On my knees before three gravestones. My family's graves. It cannot get any more factual than this. I fall forward on my hands and knees. *Tell them.* I ease myself down, my face to the earth, sprawling my arms wide, my legs, trying to touch them all. Trying to hold them all. Mira sits down next to me and Seth. Even Aidan. And a noise comes out of my throat. A husky noise, foreign and frightening. Hands tighten on mine. Another on my back. *We'll be with you.* The noises string together, like a rattling chain, and my throat jumps again and again. Real. Mother. Father. Gavin. All the things I never said. All the things I wanted to. And finally one word.

"Good-bye."

Again and again. To each of them. *Good-bye, good-bye, good-bye.* "I'm sorry I didn't say good-bye." Tears mix with soil and grass, my face pressed to the earth, hoping they hear, hoping they know, hoping they understand. Hoping that for one day, one fair, once-in-a-lifetime day, they know that I wanted to say good-bye.

I close my eyes. I float into their world, float through earth, gravel, coffin, and time. I inhabit their space, nestle in like I am there, where I should have been all along—soft, warm, safe—in their world, together, and their perspective becomes mine. I look up and see what they see, earth, stones, sky, branches, and Destiny. Their Destiny. Mother reaching up through soil and time to brush away my hair and coo in my ear. *My sweet Destiny, my baby. I never wanted to leave you.* Father reaching out and wiping my cheeks. *You're my big girl. You'll be fine.* Baby Gavin reaching, reaching and connecting with my little finger, gripping tight and smiling. *Good-bye*, they whisper. *Good-bye*. I see the Destiny they see. No longer seven, afraid, and alone. I am not alone. Today I have touched other hands and other lives. And my family is happy—happy because they know I understand. Happy because they know I will be all right. Happy because now they have been able to say good-bye too. I am theirs, always and forever theirs, and moving on doesn't mean leaving them behind. My fingers interlace tight with theirs, not wanting to let go. *But you must*, Mother whispers.

And I do.

I feel hands on my back. My arms. I float back to the world I still belong to. Mira, Aidan, and Seth are still with me like they promised. Even though I have said good-bye, I am not alone. I push up from the ground and sit on Mother's grave like I am sitting in her lap. I wipe away the bits of grass and dirt that cling to my arms. I turn to look at Seth, who is sitting beside me. He reaches out and brushes something from my nose and smiles. "You're a mess."

"I know," I answer. "That's what people have been telling me for years."

Aidan pulls a clean handkerchief from his pocket and holds it out to me. "No, he means—"

"I know what he means, Aidan." I take the handkerchief from him. "Thank you," I whisper.

I wipe the grime from my cheeks. Even with all the dirt smudging my face, for the first time in my life I don't feel like a mess. There is nothing mysterious or magical about the truth. It is simply there, cold and hard and large and unforgiving. No wonder I ran from it. But now it is facing me instead of chasing me, and that makes all the difference. The noise it made at my back was far more frightening.

I feel their stares, waiting for more answers. *This far*. There is no point in holding back now.

"Your nose," Aidan says. "Blow."

I follow his instructions. The sound is loud and harsh in the empty cemetery and quite nearly funny. I would laugh, but I don't think the others are there yet.

"It's getting late." Seth stands and helps me to my feet.

"Wait!" Mira kicks off her shoes and runs back to the car. She returns with the bouquet of sunflowers and the peacock feather and places them in my arms. "I knew when we got these, there was a good reason. I just didn't know what it was until now." She doesn't need to say what they are for. I turn and face the graves again. I brush the peacock feather against my cheek. It's as soft as a baby blanket. And blue. Blue for a baby boy. I lay it on Gavin's grave. I divide the bouquet in half and lay the first bunch on Father's grave. If flowers can smile, then these do. A smile for Father, the smile he wanted. I take the second bunch and whisper into them, a whisper from me to Mother, and I lay them down for her. She whispers back, *That's my good girl.*

I turn to the others. Their stony faces are more than I can bear.

"How's that for a secret?" I say.

Aidan is happy for the out. "Way better than the baboon heart."

Mira smiles. "Bonus points. Beats all of ours."

Seth doesn't say anything. He just looks at me and nods, and I want to say something else that is light and distant to turn the attention away from what has just happened, so I can be invisible for just a moment longer, but that time has long passed and I feel the careful layering of their gazes warm and tight about me.

I look away, squinting to the west at the last pinch of orange sun between two hills, and in that same instant, the sun vanishes, gone from view but leaving in its wake brilliant streaks of pink. The breeze is still. The music quiets. Gone.

34

CHANCE. IT WEAVES THROUGH our lives like a golden thread, sometimes knotting, tangling, and breaking along the way. Loose threads are left hanging, but the in and out, the back and forth continues, the weaving goes on. It doesn't stop, even if that is exactly what you want it to do.

The vagaries bunch up and change your life. And you adjust accordingly. You have no choice. But what do you do when chance comes along yet again and unravels the woof and warp of your existence that you've learned to survive by? How do you learn a new way of living? A new way of talking? A new way of thinking? Too much has been woven into you to leave it all behind.

And yet.

You must.

Because chance, a fair day, and three friends have made it so.

35

My parents and Gavin are dead.

Dead.

The word transforms me. Today, in an instant, in the nakedness of a moment, my life is changed. Just as it was ten years ago. Today chance has played with me again, but in a different way. An unattended car. Trash duty. Meticulous Miss Boggs miscounting her tests. A well-timed bloody nose. An annoying teacher who made me voice what I want. A fair day.

How would one fair day make a difference?

I had no clear answer for Mr. Nestor this morning, but my guesses all proved to be true. Hope, belief, justice, order, courage, power, redemption. But mostly it gives you wholeness. The broken and loose threads of your life finally blend in with the sound ones and create the texture of who you are. Tattered but whole. And maybe if you could see the back side of anyone's life, they would all have a degree of fraying.

With the setting of the sun, the temperature has dropped. By the time we get to the bottom of the hill, it is dark. Mira shivers. So do I. I pull Lucky closer.

"There's a place up there to pull over," Seth says. "I'll see if I can figure out how to get the top up." I see a barn ahead, not far off the road, a lamp at the peak of the roof creating a circle of light below.

Mira is biding her time. I know. They all are. The questions will come soon. The space they give me won't last long. Past protocol has been shattered. I have opened a door and explanations are necessary. I have already surmised they will be lengthy and painful and awkward. But necessary. I want them to know everything. I want them to know I'm not crazy. Seth turns at the dirt drive that leads to the barn and parks under the light. It casts a dim warm glow on us.

"Let's go inside," Mira says. She is already out of the car and venturing in before we can respond. A light inside flips on. Seth grabs Lucky and we follow. We find her sitting on a bale of hay, settled in like she is waiting for something. Waiting for me. The biding time is over. Better now in the light where I can see their faces and know what they think of me.

36

"I CAN'T IMAGINE what it must have been like for you," Mira says.

We sit in a circle on a bed of straw, knee to knee, leaning against the bales of hay at our backs. I look at the past like I am looking at moving pictures of someone else, and I tell them everything—everything I can remember from my seven-year-old perspective and everything Mr. Gardian told me along the way too.

I watch their faces as I speak, looking for flinching, glances between them, or other signs that I should stop, but I see none, so I go on. I tell them how the doctors thought that seeing my parents die right before my eyes had left me a bit touched. I admit to them that for a time it probably had. The truth was too hard to accept. But I was never crazy. Not like I heard some nurses whisper. *Poor thing, maybe it would have been better for her to be on the plane with them.* All the things they thought I didn't hear, but I did. And then all the defenses I created to help me cope, like saying my parents abandoned me.

"So you made up that story?" Seth asks.

"Not exactly. That version was just there in my head. A coping mechanism, the doctors called it. And that became the truth of my world. If my parents had only abandoned me, no matter how despicable, then maybe . . ."

"Then maybe one day they could come back," Mira finishes.

"Something like that."

Mira leans forward and picks at her shoes. "I know this isn't the same, but I sort of did something similar when"—she looks up. "I don't think I've ever mentioned it, but my parents are divorced. It was a nasty one." She looks back down at her shoes. "And when we were going through all the court battles, I actually pretended they weren't my parents. I imagined that they were horrible fakes and that my real parents—the nice, reasonable ones—would come back and smooth the whole mess out. That all I wanted was for everything to be smoothed out and go back to the way it was."

She looks up and smiles. "I pretended like that for about three months until they forbade me to call them Harold and Vivian anymore. Those weren't even their names. I pulled them out of thin air. Names of strangers. Because that's what they were to me." Her smile vanishes. "When they banished the names, well, by then I already knew the reasonable parents were never returning, so I went back to calling them Mum and Pop. But that fantasy got me through a tough patch." She weaves her hands together and looks at me with a hesitant sideways glance. "So I understand why you would make something like that up, Des. When the world's unreasonable, sometimes it seems like the only thing to do."

I look at Mira, staring straight into her eyes like I have never done before, looking in a way that most would deem impolite or uncomfortable, but it is neither. It makes me wonder why I have never done it before. I finally nod. "That's right, Mira. We do what we have to do."

"A fantasy for a few months is one thing," Aidan says, "but you never stopped. Didn't you have, um, like, *therapy*?"

I shake my head and grin. "You don't know the half of it, Aidan. Poor Mr. Farrell. He was my father's best friend and attorney, but I didn't really know him because he lived far away in the city. I was so young and he was just a shadowy figure who came in and out of our lives. I still remember when he came to the house and tried to explain to me that he had been named my guardian and—"

"Your *guardian*. So that's why you call him that," Seth says.

I smile. "I was logical, even then." I tell them about my move hundreds of miles away to the city where Mr. Gardian lived, but I didn't do well there. Not that Mr. Gardian didn't try, but he was an inexperienced bachelor and I was an angry, mixed-up seven-year-old. He thought that going back to the house in Langdon might help, so he actually moved back there with me, hiring yet another nanny to help him. But I didn't like strangers in my house, where my mother and father and Gavin should have been. When we returned there, I only got worse. I withdrew and stopped talking and eating. I remember Mr. Gardian always on the phone, always taking me to doctors, often taking me to the park just to get away. Finally it was decided I needed a special school that was all about therapy.

"It took a while," I say. "But it eventually helped. Some. I'm at least talking, aren't I? But all the therapy in the world might be able to convince you of the truth, but it doesn't change how your brain has learned to work. Or maybe how I chose for it to work."

Mira leans back and folds her arms. "But why did Mr. Farrell bounce you around from school to school? It wasn't your parents who kept switching you, like you told Mrs. Wicket."

"You eavesdrop far more than I give you credit for, Mira."

She shrugs and grins. "Sorry."

"I kept switching because—" I remember all the long talks with counselors where I listened but didn't speak. "When you witness your whole family die and you think it's your fault, you"—my breath shimmies in my lungs and I feel my cheeks grow hot. I slide my hands beneath my knees and hug them. "You think that maybe there's something bad about you. Something that makes people disappear. It makes you afraid—"

"You were afraid to get close to anyone again," Seth finishes for me.

I nod. "When I found myself looking forward to seeing someone the next day and the next at a school, I'd do something to put an end to it. By the time I was ten, I knew exactly what sorts of behaviors would have me packing my bags the next day. It got to the point that when the boarding school called, Mr. Gardian knew just what was coming. He never showed his displeasure." I turn and look at Mira. "I suppose with him it was sort of like bonus points too. After what I had been through, he thought I had earned a certain dispensation, I guess, and he just accepted that I was destined to have my . . . difficult periods."

"You said you thought it was your fault. Why would you think that?" Seth asks.

I look at Seth. Didn't I already make that clear at the cemetery? I refused to say good-bye. Ever since that day, I've thought of that word over and over again and the difference it might have made—a fraction of a second, and a lifetime of wondering kind of difference. "When I didn't say good-bye," I tell him, "I felt like I helped to make all the seconds add up wrong."

Aidan snorts. "That's craz"—he catches himself. "I mean—"

"Of course it's a crazy way to think, Aidan," I say. "But sometimes the way life plays out is crazy too. At the very least, it defies explanation. Maybe one insanity balances out the other."

Aidan nods.

"Why were your parents going somewhere without you in the first place?" Mira asks.

"They had to. My baby brother, Gavin, was born with a hole in his heart. I didn't really understand back then. My parents tried to explain it, but he looked healthy to me. I remember his tiny perfect fingers. But when he cried, he'd lose his breath, and I remember my mother doing anything to keep him happy. There was a special doctor they wanted to see, but he was very busy. He was booked for months."

"Except for your birthday," Mira says, holding her cheeks like she is astonished all over again.

"That's right. My birthday and my mother's. And that's where the other things went wrong. It was the wrong day, by all accounts." I explain about the appointment changes, flight changes, and that my parents weren't even supposed to be at that airport in the first place. My father had planned to fly his own plane, but Gavin's appointment was more important than convenience or birthdays. It was all so last-minute. Mr. Gardian relayed some of this information to me over the years; some I knew because I was there, but other bits came from therapists and counselors who unwittingly helped me piece together a warped logic of numbers and timing. And of course the worst timing of all happened right before my eyes.

"Another plane that was coming in lost an engine," I explain and then correct myself. "No, it didn't just lose it—it was a catastrophic failure. The engine exploded, and they were so close to landing, the pilot didn't have a chance to veer away. He flew straight into my parents' plane. Esme, my babysitter, pulled me away from the window, but it was too late. I saw everything. What are the chances? The day that brought my mother took her away again, and everything that could go wrong, did. Maybe it is the Law of Truly Large Numbers. But when it happens to you, it doesn't feel like a statistic."

Seth sighs. "And now today. Escrow closing on the same day as they died."

"That part wasn't a coincidence. That was my doing. Mr. Gardian has wanted to sell the house for years, but he always deferred to me, and I always said no. I know everyone thought he was crazy for listening to a child, but he did. One time a Realtor even contacted me directly. Mr. Gardian was furious. I guess he thought that so much had been taken away from me, he wanted to give me some power back. He loved my parents. I never really stopped to think about how much he had lost too. A few months ago, he asked me about the house again. He told me it wasn't wise to leave it standing empty. He said someone should be living in it. A family. I finally agreed. On one condition—"

"That the sale was final on October 19," Aidan finishes.

"I thought that maybe—" I look away.

"The numbers again," Seth says.

I nod. "I still"—I look at my open palms in my lap—"I still hoped there was a key. Something I had missed. A way to turn back time, maybe. If everything added up just right, the way everything had added up just wrong that day . . ." I look away from my hands into the rafters of the barn. "I know it's not possible. *I know*. But sometimes the world makes no sense anyway."

"It's unfair."

"It stinks."

"Sometimes you—"

"Yes," I whisper.

Seth exhales a puffy breath of air. "You still worry, don't you? About today. That it will take you like it did your mother."

I am caught off guard by his bluntness. I've never spoken it aloud, fearing that saying it might make it true, but he's right. "I used to be terrified," I finally admit. "In fact I hardly breathed on my birthdays, so Mr. Gardian let all my teachers and counselors know that my birthday was not to be mentioned or celebrated because it would send me into such a downward spiral."

I smile, realizing how far I have come. "Last year Mr. Gardian actually tested the waters and sent me a birthday card, and it didn't send me into a complete catatonic state. I suppose that's another sign of acceptance or getting better. Maybe I've just finally accepted that I don't know why things happen the way they do. Sometimes it seems there's pattern and purpose, and other times it's all sheer chaos, and I suppose the day I die could fall into either category." I lean back and cross my legs. "But whatever it is, chaos or design, it's the only game in town, right? It's not like we have a choice. Take the mixed bag or take nothing at all. And I'm tired of taking nothing at all."

"It's a lot like a bowl of mixed nuts, don't you think?" Mira says. "I hate the cashews, but I eat them to be polite. It would be wrong to pick through and just take the best nuts."

Best nuts? We stare silently at Mira. She blushes.

"I'm sorry. That's a terrible analogy. It's not like you could choose the, well, you know, everything." She looks down at her lap.

Seth laughs and throws a handful of hay at Mira. "It's as good an analogy as any, Mira. And I think a nuts analogy is especially apropos for Des."

Mira's face shoots up, her eyes wide. Aidan follows suit, staring at Seth, his mouth open, speechless. I look at Seth too, his eyes just the opposite of theirs, narrowing slightly. Smooth. Like a grin. Pushing me. Like I am a normal person.

The silence and tension grow to comical proportions, and I finally grab two handfuls of hay and throw them at Seth, shattering the strained silence. Laughter sputters from my throat, and Mira joins me, laughing and throwing hay too, and soon we are all laughing, hay in our laps, hay in our hair, hay raining down handful after handful. We hold our stomachs, gulping for breath, laughing beyond reason, laughing at the absurdities of ourselves and life.

And then Seth nudges my foot with his, like a private nod from him to me, a small action the others don't notice, and for a moment I feel intoxicated, connected and belonging to this world like I have never felt before.

Our laughter quiets. Mira wipes her eyes. Aidan blows his nose.

And I do something bold, something I've never done. I nudge Seth's foot back and mouth, *Thank you*. His eyes crease slightly and his head barely moves, the smallest up-and-down motion.

"This was the best day ever," Mira says, wiggling her red platform pumps in front of her. "Seth got his dog, Aidan talked to the president, and Des finally got to say goodbye, but I think right now is the best part of the whole day." Mira's face is a picture of contentment. We are nestled together on a bed of hay, a tight circle, where secrets and distance have been patted away, no wrinkles for Mira to worry over, no innuendo, no harsh voices or tense glances to be averted. Just the moment and her flashy platform pumps wiggling like everything is right with the world.

And maybe for this one moment, it is.

37

IT IS TIME TO RETURN to Hedgebrook. No one has yet stated the obvious.

We are doomed. At least I am.

It has been the fair day I wished for, but the day is not over. If the snipped ponytail wasn't enough, the appropriated car and corrupting of three formerly model students will certainly have me shipped off by morning, this time quite possibly to a place with striped uniforms. And the irony is, now for once, I desperately want to stay. I have a reason to stay. But I know a day like today can't last forever. Even I am not that delusional.

I hold Lucky while Aidan and Seth pull up the leather top of the car. Mira supervises, pointing out the levers to secure it.

"There!" Seth says, pushing down the last clamp. "That

should make it a little warmer." We are all shivering now. Late October is no time to be outside at night and coatless.

"Our jackets!" Mira says. "Let's get them out of the trunk."

Hedgebrook and our jackets seem a lifetime away. I had forgotten them, but the boring navy blazers are welcome now. We huddle near the trunk while Seth opens it. A small bulb illuminates the inside and Seth pulls out the bag from Babs's store that holds our clothes and dispenses the jackets. We eagerly put them on. He points to the back of the trunk at a large cardboard box. "I wonder what's in it? I saw it this morning, but that was when I thought this was your car."

"Maybe there's food? Cookies or something," Aidan says hopefully.

"Should we peek?" Mira asks.

"Stealing a few cookies won't add much to our problems at this point," Seth says. He reaches in and slides it toward us. The top flaps are interlocked, and when Seth pulls on one, they all pop up. He peers in and lifts some tissue. "No cookies. Not even close."

Mira nudges him aside and looks in too. "Dolls?" She reaches in and pulls one out.

My heart jumps. I recognize the flowing green gown. A

Scarlett O'Hara Madame Alexander doll. I thrust Lucky into Aidan's arms and step past him to look inside. I pull the dolls out, one after the other. Little Red Riding Hood! Cissy in her aqua gown! Lady of Spain! All of them. All the dolls that were missing from my shelf. "These are mine!"

"What?" Seth asks.

"These are my dolls! My collection! The ones that were missing from my shelf!"

"That's impossible," Aidan says.

I spot a folded piece of paper in the box and pull it out. I open it and hold it close to the glowing trunk bulb. I read it aloud.

"I thought you would want to keep these. They shouldn't take up much room at Hedgebrook.—EF."

I shake my head. I still don't understand. "How—"

"The glove box!" Seth shouts. "Check the glove box!" But he is already racing to it himself. He shuffles through it, money and paper falling to the floor of the car, until he finally emerges with a white envelope smaller than his palm. He hands it to me. The dim barn light is enough for me to read the neatly printed letters on the front.

Destiny.

My fingers shake as I pull out a pink card. The front has a tiny glittered white birthday cake on it. I open it.

I read it aloud to the others.

"Happy Birthday, Destiny. I think it's time for you to celebrate. These wheels come with an instructor and lessons. I've included some cash for fuel. I hope you like it. And I hope you still like pink. Love, Mr. Farrell."

"It's for your birthday," Seth says, like he has unraveled a great mystery.

I look up at him. I can't think. He grabs my shoulders and says again, this time very slowly, "He gave you this car for your birthday, Destiny. It was yours all along."

"That's right!" Aidan says. "Back at the house, Mr. Farrell said he had sent a little something for her to Hedgebrook."

"I'll say it's a little something!" Mira chimes in. "A big little something!" She and Aidan climb into the back seat with a seemingly newfound appreciation for the car now that it's mine. Mira runs her hand over the chrome door handles.

"It's my car," I say, still stunned. I open my door and get in. I slide my hand across the leather seat. It is not the extravagance of the car that stuns me. It is the thought put into its choice. The color, the model, all different and quirky like me. Mr. Gardian used great care in selecting it and also in its delivery. I am still retracing the steps I took when I stumbled upon it this morning. The messenger who brought it must have stepped away for just a brief moment, perhaps looking for directions. It was supposed to be a surprise. A gift from Mr. Gardian. I've had years of kindness and patience from him, kindness I could never fully accept, turning away compliments and encouragement, keeping him at a distance as I did everyone else, but he never wavered in his duty to care for me or failed to pay attention to the subtle cues of my likes and dislikes. Mother and Father chose well. My car. I finger the hole that Lucky chewed in the middle of the seat, and Seth winces.

"It's fine," I say. "Just as it is."

"We could all chip in—"

"Seth, I am probably the wealthiest orphan in the country—at least I will be when I turn twenty-one. If I wanted to fix it a hundred times over, I could. Maybe one day I will. But for now I'll think of it as a souvenir of this day."

"I knew you had to be loaded," Aidan says. "I just didn't know *how* loaded."

"But there's one thing I still don't get," Mira says,

leaning over the back of my seat. "Why didn't you go live with your aunt Edie instead of Mr. Farrell? She *is* a blood relative, after all."

My stomach twists. Aunt Edie was the one detail I avoided. I look at Seth and then back to Mira. How much can one person be expected to give up in one day? My perfect aunt. The one who talked for me when I couldn't. The one who wanted me. The one Mr. Gardian tolerated because he knew I needed her. I feel my lips part, but I can't force any words between them.

"It's all right." Mira plops back in her seat. "You don't have to tell. You've shared enough secrets today."

"There is no Aunt Edie," I blurt out. "There never was."

Seth watches me carefully. I am ashamed that I still held back. The car fills with awkward silence.

"What about this morning?" Aidan finally asks. "The note that said she couldn't come."

"That was from me. I called the front office and left the message. I've always covered for Aunt Edie, to explain her absences."

"But you just said there is no Aunt Edie. How can you cover for someone who doesn't exist?"

I turn fully around in my seat to look at Aidan. "Listen, Aidan. For *me* she did exist. She was exactly the kind of aunt I needed—one who could never be taken away from me. She was someone I wasn't afraid to love."

My final word, *love*, stops him just as he is about to reply. Dipping into emotions is indeed a sticky business, something that I am not used to, either. The only person I allowed that emotion was Aunt Edie, and now she's outed. I turn around and stare straight ahead into the darkness.

"At least the unmailed letters make more sense now," Aidan says quietly.

Mira leans forward and pats my shoulder. "I think it's okay to have an Aunt Edie. Ingenious, really. I wish I had thought of it. Except I would have named her Aunt Lucy. I've always liked that name."

Yes, every wrinkle patted out. I smile. "Thanks, Mira. I think Lucy would have been a fine name too. I may save it for a future use."

Seth searches through his pockets for the key. "No future use, okay? There's plenty of real people for you to"—he stops his fidgeting and glances at me.

"Yes?" I say.

"Found it," he answers, pulling the key out of his left pocket.

I hear Mira smack the seat. "I still can't believe this gorgeous car is yours."

"I can," Aidan says, lifting Lucky over the seat and placing him between me and Seth. "Today I could believe almost anything. She stole her own car."

"But technically that's impossible," Mira corrects. "You can't steal something you own. So she's off the hook. We're all off the hook."

Seth starts the motor and gets back on the road.

"Off the hook for the car maybe, but not for taking off," Aidan says. "You know how the headmaster is about making examples of rule breakers."

As much as I hate to admit it, Aidan is thoroughly and completely right. There will be consequences to pay, severe ones for me, since I am a repeat offender, and certainly stern consequences for the others. But this cloud hanging over us can't seem to shadow the wonder of the day. Not for any of us. Even Aidan. I hear it in his voice. He talks again about peeing next to the president, sharing his ideas, and maybe even having Congress name a bill after him. Mira has nestled in close on Aidan's side of the seat, her head boldly resting on his shoulder, and she tells him she believes anything is possible, maybe even a bill named the Aidan Vacation Act. And maybe I believe it too.

Today defies explanation, but for me, life has never

been explainable. It's been a lopsided, illogical, messy affair, where answers are in short supply, but maybe that's the way it is for everyone. Sometimes the fairness is all bunched up in one place, and all the injustice is bunched up in another, and sometimes it is all bunched up in the most improbable ways, but whatever you get, wherever you are, there are still the moments that pin you to this world when you'd rather float away. Small, in-between moments, where there is magic and purpose and design and they are so perfectly beautiful they ache. Like all the in-between moments of today. Maybe the good guy doesn't always win. And maybe fairness doesn't always land where it should. But today felt good, deliciously and wonderfully good, just like I told Mr. Nestor this morning. And sometimes that's enough.

A three-quarter dollop of moon and a sky that has split open with stars sprinkle silver light on the landscape that we traveled past this morning. Only occasionally is the scenery recognizable. The brilliantly colored trees that stole our attention earlier today must now take a back seat to a sky that touches the earth with its own brilliance. Aidan and Mira have fallen into whispers and giggles with intermittent shrieks from either one pointing out shooting stars. Seth has pulled Lucky closer, or perhaps it was

Lucky who nuzzled in of his own accord. I wish I was as brave as Lucky.

As we pass the sign to Drivby, Mira sighs and says, "Before we get back, tell us another one, Des. One more."

"Another what?"

"One of those amazing stories that you know. You know, the ones filled with chance."

"Yeah, let's hear another one," Aidan agrees.

Seth looks at me and even in the dark I can see his eyebrows rise in surprise. Aidan requesting one of my stories truly marks a once-in-a-lifetime sort of day.

"All right," I say, not even sure I have another interesting one to share. But then . . . I realize I do. "Once there were four young people, all exceedingly bright—one especially so—and they set off on a road trip. By all accounts, it should have been a disaster. It was that kind of day. A day where things had gone wrong from the start for each of them. But there was something stirring that day, a momentum that took hold of them, something they couldn't control or hope to explain. And the truly amazing thing—the coincidental part of this story—is that not one of them tried. They just let themselves be swept along by something outside of themselves. And one of them . . . one of them . . . found some things along the road that she had lost—things she didn't even know she was missing. Things that you can't hold or touch, like forgiveness, acceptance, and maybe even justice, and that made it all the more amazing because invisible things are so much harder to find. But her friends helped her and four pairs of eyes are always better than one. Four is the perfect number.

"And there was a dog. I can't forget that part of the story. A beautiful dog named Lucky, but no one knew he was a dog, except for the one who named him. He could see beneath the woolly surface all the way down to the dog's true nature. He was even able to make Lucky forget about what others thought he was. He was just a dog like any other, even if he didn't look like a normal one.

"And then the most truly amazing and unexplainable thing happened—*the day never ended*. It went on and on forever, and none of them could ever forget it because it was always with them. Even when they finally had to say good-bye, the day went on. They called it The Day That Never Ended. I know it's hard to believe, but it's true. Cross my baboon heart."

Mira sighs. "That's a good one, Des," she says. "I think that's my favorite story of all."

38

WE ARE STILL A MILE from Hedgebrook when Seth notes the traffic.

"I've never seen this many cars on this road," he says. I hear the rise in his voice. It is a question. Mira and Aidan are sitting up leaning over the back of our seats now to get a better view of the stream of cars.

"What do you think's going on?" Mira asks.

No one answers. I am sure Aidan's and Seth's imaginations are running as wild as mine. Is there a manhunt going on for us? A massive search? Did they surmise that I finally snapped and fear what I might have done to my classmates? Is this day going to live up to its history, after all? How fast am I going to be whisked away from Hedgebrook?

As we get closer, Mira points to the helicopters. There are two. At least. And a glow coming from Hedgebrook like it has been turned into a landing strip. Lights like we have never seen. My grip tightens on my knees.

Seth utters an appropriate word for the situation and then apologizes. Aidan repeats it. No apology.

As we turn into the long driveway to Hedgebrook we have to maneuver past cars, vans, and camera crews.

"Channel Eight!" Aidan says.

Seth's head is swiveling. "World News?"

I grab the steering wheel. "Watch the road!"

"I think we've been missed," Mira says.

Throngs of students fill the lawns. They are all dressed in their Saturday casuals, even though it is not the weekend. This is definitely not a planned Hedgebrook activity. Seth parks the car at the curb outside Gaspar Hall, strictly a no-parking zone, but in the chaos it seems irrelevant. Even Aidan doesn't object.

Seth steps out and reaches back for Lucky. "Come on, fella," he says, nuzzling Lucky's face before tucking him snugly under his arm. I catch my breath. The idea of Seth having to say good-bye to Lucky is suddenly much worse than my saying good-bye to Hedgebrook. I wonder how long it will take for someone to spot us, for it all to come crashing down. We get out and make our way over to the crowds. We don't get far before Jillian and Curtis spot us and run over.

"You owe us big time!" Jillian says.

"We've been covering for you all day," Curtis adds.

"What are you talking about?" Seth asks.

Jillian reaches out and pets Lucky and then kisses his nose like he's a baby. "Darling," she says. His stubby little tail wags. "We saw you leave in the car, remember? But ever since the meteor hit this morning, Mrs. Wicket has been checking off students—"

"A meteor?" Aidan says. "What the—?"

"Well, they think that's what it was. But they're very rare. Over there—"

We are all walking in the direction Jillian pointed before she can even finish.

"That's what it was!" Mira says.

"What *what* was?" Aidan is obviously disconcerted that Mira is on to something before he is and is hurrying to stay close by her side.

"That sound! This morning! It wasn't a negative giant!"

"Positive giant," Aidan corrects her. "But it could have been."

We squeeze through people until we are stopped by a

yellow tape. "Could have been, but not this time, Cowboy," Mira says. "Nooo, sir!"

We stare at the quad, speechless. The green lawn is littered with dirt and rocks and men in white uniforms carrying scientific instruments and reporters daring to get a closer look. In the center, exactly where the grotesque statue of Argus Hedgebrook once stood, is a gaping crater at least twenty feet across, like Argus was the bull's-eye of a precisely drawn target. The first thought that runs through my mind is justice at last for Argus Hedgebrook, his embarrassing arthritic pose finally laid to rest deep within the earth. I look at the others, their jaws hanging open just like mine. We begin laughing at the same time, like we are all hit at once with the absurd fairness of it all.

The momentum. It is still with us.

"Even old man Argus got his share of fair today!" Mira says.

"Won't have me to make fun of anymore!" Aidan throws his hand out in a mocking arthritic gesture.

"The crater is quite an improvement," I add.

Our laughter gradually subsides, except for Seth's. He is still laughing hysterically, tears rolling down his cheeks.

"Seth?" Mira says.

"This morning," he gurgles.

Aidan puts his hand on Seth's shoulder. "You all right, buddy?"

Seth's head rears back and he howls. "Me. The statue."

"Oh, my God," I say.

"What?" Mira's head spins sharply toward me. "Will you please tell us what's going on with him? Is he all right?"

Seth regains enough composure to string more than two words together and blurts out, "That's where I was hiding!" And promptly goes into another blubbering fit of laughter.

"What's he talking about?" Aidan says, grabbing Lucky out of Seth's arms like he's afraid Seth may drop him.

"This morning Seth was hiding out under the statue trying to avoid trash duty."

"And Destiny came and got me," Seth says in a gulping breath. The laughter drains away as quickly as it came, and he looks at me, his face definitely several shades whiter than it was just a moment ago. "She saved my life. If she hadn't come and got me—"

"You'd be flatter than a pancake!" Mira gasps.

"Yeah . . . I guess I would." His gaze is fixed on me, and mine on him. Everything shifts to slow motion. "You saved my life," he repeats. He takes a step toward me.

"The day's come full circle, then, hasn't it?" I answer. He steps closer. And I think, right then, right there, even in front of all these people, if Seth leaned forward and bent his head down to mine, I would—

"There you are!"

The world is jarred back to its quick pace. Mrs. Wicket is breathless, her hair a disarrayed jumble. She blows out a well-directed puff of air to shoo a stray silver wisp from her eyes. "I've been three steps behind you all day! Seems every time I would arrive somewhere, I would be told I just missed you. I included you in the head count the headmaster wanted since Jillian, Curtis, and Ben had all said they had seen you, but I wanted to see you for myself too."

"We're here, Mrs. Wicket, safe and sound," I say.

She smiles, clearly relieved. "Yes, you are."

Baaaa!

Aidan shoves Lucky back into Seth's arms. "He wants you."

"What have we here?" Mrs. Wicket asks.

The color springs back to Seth's face. "My lamb, Mrs. Wicket. But he's very well trained. I promise he—"

"A lamb! Seth! How did you know? The headmaster will be delighted!"

"Huh?"

"You know he's been wanting to restore the old livestock pen to its previous use. He's been rumbling about that project for months. As he puts it, he's tired of the pen being used as a 'den for questionable activities.' He will be so pleased when he sees this adorable lamb. An excellent first addition and a great way to get his project off the ground! He'll be so excited. Smart thinking, Seth. I wouldn't be a bit surprised if he gave you extra credit! Must run now. Don't forget, curfew in ten minutes." Her eyes roll and she shakes her head. "Today has been unbelievable!" She gives Lucky a quick pat and is off on more business.

Extra credit. Unbelievable indeed. From start to finish.

She is already several feet away when I run after her. "Mrs. Wicket!" I call. She stops abruptly, and I nearly tumble into her. "I have a quick question."

"Yes, dear?"

"I was wondering about Mr. Nestor, the visiting calculus teacher who was here—"

"Mr. who?"

"Nestor. He teaches calculus."

"We have no Mr. Nestor here at Hedgebrook, dear. Visiting or otherwise. Are you sure you have the name right?

Or maybe it was a reporter you spoke to? There's been so much confusion today!"

A reporter? No. Perhaps the messenger who delivered the car and was trying to cover his identity? Maybe. A figment of my imagination? Possibly. Or perhaps someone else? Or something else? Something. "Of course. A reporter," I answer. "That was probably it. Good night, Mrs. Wicket."

I join the others and we begin walking back to Carroll Hall. When we are a safe distance away from the crowd, Mira raises a victory fist and whispers, "No one missed us!"

"We're off the hook," Aidan adds.

"And I'll be able to stay at Hedgebrook."

"And I'm still alive," Seth says. "With Lucky *and* extra credit."

We pause at the hallway where we must part ways, Mira and I to our wing of the dorm, and Seth and Aidan to theirs.

"It's like we were never gone," Seth says.

"Oh, we were gone, all right," Mira replies, admiring her red pumps.

"What happened today?" Aidan asks, like he is freshly stunned.

We are all dazed, thrown yet another curve from what

we were expecting. I look at my three road-trip renegades. I have no answers. I only know that in a vast and infinite universe, somehow today, I feel less small, less forgotten, less afraid, and infinitely more ready for another day.

"Life, Aidan," I finally say. "And trying to explain it is like trying to explain a lambadoodle to someone who can only see a woolly sheep."

Mira lightly pokes Aidan on his chest. "Pay attention, Cowboy. It's The Day That Never Ended. Remember?"

"And it's also the day Destiny Faraday smiled at least a dozen times," Seth adds.

Aidan scratches his head and smiles. "Did hell freeze over?" Mira punches him, and they fall into giggles and close muted conversation.

"Could be," Seth answers, even though Aidan is no longer listening, and right there, Seth bends over and kisses my cheek. "See you at breakfast," he says and walks away with Lucky still asleep in his arms.

39

I LOOK AT THE CALENDAR. October 20. Its own once-in-a-lifetime kind of day. I smooth my hand over the page. I don't tear it or crumple it. I don't want this day to pass before its time. Next to the calendar is a pink sealed envelope. I slide it from my dresser and tuck it into my pocket, to be mailed later, my long-overdue letter to Mr. Gardian.

There is shuffling in the hall. Mira pokes her head in. "Breakfast, Des."

Like I don't know.

"On my way, Mira."

"I'll save you a seat between me and *Seth*."

"Mira!" I turn sharply, then stop. A saved seat next to Seth. Certainly not the end of the world. Not at all. "Like I said, on my way," I answer.

I tuck my sheet beneath the mattress, folding the corner the way Aunt Edie—the way Mrs. Wicket—showed me on my first day. Routine, the lifeblood of Hedgebrook. At least it was. Today Seth will be at breakfast, and I will sit next to him. And today—who knows?—maybe Cook will even stir the lumps from the oatmeal.

"On my way," I whisper again, this time to no one but myself, and I hurry to join the others.

Acknowledgments

I OWE ENORMOUS THANKS to Jill Rubalcaba, Jessica Pearson, Melissa Wyatt, Marlene Perez, Karen and Ben Beiswenger, Shirley Harazin, Catherine Atkins, Lisa Firke, Amy Butler, Laura Weiss, Kristina Cliff Evans, Lisa Harkrader, Cynthia Lord, Amy McAuley, Nancy Werlin, and Amanda Jenkins, for reading first drafts, snips, and wild calls for help, answering questions from the bizarre to the mundane, and offering an endless amount of support and encouragement.

I am grateful to the amazing staff at Henry Holt—too many to name and I know I would surely leave someone out—but they make the publishing process a delight with their professionalism, wisdom, and enthusiasm. So many thanks to you all.

Rosemary Stimola is one brilliant lady, and I am so grateful she is my agent. Thanks for all the hand-holding, advice, hard work, and friendship, Ro.

My editor, Kate Farrell, continues to be the most supportive and wise editor a writer could ask for. I am blessed. Thank you, Kate.

An ocean of gratitude to my precious family, Dennis, Karen, Jessica, and Ben, who are a never-ending source of inspiration for me. They make the ride wild, fun, sometimes bumpy, and always interesting. My infinite love and thanks go to them.